DATE DUE

DEATH OF A CROW

DEATH OF A CROW

A NOVEL OF SUSPENSE

Ursula Curtiss

DODD, MEAD & COMPANY
New York, New York

1 2 3 4 5 6 7 8 9 10

Library of Congress Cataloging in Publication Data

Curtiss, Ursula Reilly.
  Death of a crow.

  I. Title.
PS3505.U915D4   1983   813'.54   82-19951
ISBN 0-396-08130-4

DEATH OF A CROW

One

When Laura had excused herself to go briefly upstairs, the
dozen or so friends and relatives who had come back to the
house after the funeral—casket closed because no art could
have restored Bernard for public viewing—busied themselves, glasses in hand, with the usual postcemetery talk.

"Did you see that troll in the gorgeous white suede
coat? What a waste."

"Frank Eakins looked ready for the next plot. How old
is he, anyway?"

"That FBI type had to be a detective. I felt like a shop-
lifter all during the prayers."

"Laura bore up very well, considering."

Yes, they all agreed, she had; scarcely flinching even
when a press photographer, supposedly banned from the
graveside services, had called suddenly, "Oh, Mrs.
Fourte?" and materialized from behind a monument to record the startled turn of Laura's head.

"She's marvelous, really, to be putting Max down for
his nap as if nothing . . ."

Thoughtful pause in this group while human nature
took over. "When Hal went, I was shattered absolutely to
pieces. People had to *tell* me what went on the whole day
of the funeral, and that wasn't even sudden, like this."

"Suddenly, while driving." A little shiver somewhere.

"Still, you have to admire her." It had the weighing sound of suspended judgment. "Was she ever an actress, or a model? Bear in mind that I was in Europe when they were married, and on the West Coast since."

"Bernard would bite you for that, given the opportunity," said a lean man with a long head. "Laura is Robert Gillespie's daughter. He won a Pulitzer prize for a novel about owls."

"Ah, nothing but the best, as usual," murmured the shattered but well-mended widow.

"And she is astonishingly nice," said the lean man.

"And what's more," said a perimeter voice warningly, "here she comes."

Laura was still in the lilac suit she had worn under a charcoal coat on this bitterly cold day, and still paper pale; she had had neither the time nor the wish for minutes in front of the mirror with little boxes and feathery brushes. At two years of age, her stepson had no departure point for "dead," let alone "murdered," but he seemed to accept the fact that his father was irretrievably gone. It followed that he was afraid Laura would join Bernard in that unknown place, with just as little warning, and it had taken an interval of sitting quietly beside his crib, refusing the housekeeper's offer to do that, before he could be left.

The half aspirin for his low-grade fever had helped, administered in raspberry jam because tablets had a way of dissolving at the top of his throat. Laura herself had had recourse to a tranquilizer shortly before leaving for the church, and she supposed vaguely that it was still with her.

It must have been, because as she reached the bottom of the stairs in the dining room, becoming visible from one end of the living room, it was like rejoining a party with ears slightly blocked. The occasional peal of laughter was missing, but there was the same animated hum, the same little groups, either sitting or standing, of people handsomely turned out and thoroughly familiar with the house.

Julian Fourte, who might have been Bernard's twin brother although he was four years older, met Laura at once with a drink extended, and Bernard's great-aunt patted the couch beside her in imperative invitation. Although there were only the two of them—Bernard's sister was ill in Paris, and apart from that there were only cousins who didn't appear to count—it was a protective closing of the ranks around the girl who was eleven years younger than Bernard and had been married to him for only eight months.

On one level, Laura appreciated it. On another, she knew what it meant.

Her swallow of bloody mary was steadying. She said to tiny, wrinkled, imposing Catherine Fourte, "There's a buffet in the dining room. I hope everybody will gradually . . ."

Catherine cast an experienced eye over the assemblage. "In about ten minutes, I would expect. Tell me, are the police still pursuing that wicked nonsense about a hitchhiker?"

Before Laura could answer, a lull fell over the room—cigarettes being lit, glasses sipped at?—like a tide going out to reveal what it had been covering. Into it, a man's voice somewhere behind the couch said, "At least Delahanty had the grace to stay away."

"Not entirely, he was at the church. Why 'the grace'?"

The second voice was already fading, as if its owner, the Fourte lawyer, were being beckoned a discreet distance away. Homer Poe, the initiator of the cutoff exchange, was a natural talker-in-corners. Laura had asked him back to the house only because, almost doglike in his devotion to Bernard, he would be genuinely stricken at the omission and also well aware that his absence would be remarked with what could only be called mass satisfaction—although strangely enough, as if under hypnosis, people were apt to tell Homer things.

"Yes, as far as I know," said Laura to the impatient old gaze. It was a relief, in a way, not to be glossing over the facts of violent death and interment with safer subjects: the plight of Broadway musicals, skiing conditions in Stowe. "Although I've told them from the beginning that Bernard would never have stopped to pick up a hitchhiker."

It was true; even a passing acquaintance of Bernard's could have volunteered the information. He had felt so strongly on the subject as to din into Laura the habit of pressing down the lock buttons on her car for the shortest drives, even though the oldish Mustang she had brought to the marriage and insisted upon keeping could not be regarded in the same light as his custom Mercedes.

The police had clearly taken this insistence with a diplomatic grain of salt. Bernard Fourte, a very attractive thirty-nine, might have been proof against any number of knapsacked wayfarers, but what about a pretty woman in evident distress?

(Who just happened to be carrying a .22 with which to destroy him? And who had chosen to wait by the roadside instead of taking her problem to the nearest house and telephone? This was not an expanse of Arizona desert, but a pleasant, winding stretch of Connecticut.)

On the other hand, the unslued parking on the shoulder and the lack of burned-rubber tracks said that Fourte had brought the Mercedes to a considered stop, and there was no doubt whatever that he had been shot inside the car and behind the wheel.

His wallet, missing, must have come as a disappointment; a writer of checks and a user of credit cards, he seldom carried more than thirty dollars in cash. A clearly expensive gold watch was still on his wrist. It was Julian, quick witted as Bernard would have been in the midst of shock, who had remembered to report the credit cards.

Ironically, Bernard had died within two hundred yards of home.

Was that Mr. Fourte's usual route from the railroad station?

Yes.

Was that afternoon train the one he was in the habit of taking from Grand Central?

Yes. Frequently during the week, unfailingly on Fridays.

So that? . . .

It had been a mistake to sit instead of standing, because for seconds the back of the couch drew the back of Laura's dark head like a magnet. She thought with a detachment she knew to be appalling that, like most rituals which survived, this one must have its roots in practicality: not so much to comfort as to ensure that life went on in its appointed way. Small children to be tended, cows milked, wood chopped.

Here, Max slept; the oil burner went soundlessly about its business; Mrs. Wedge, who was cook as well as housekeeper, labored in the kitchen over this soberest of all challenges. Might she bring forth a mousse?

Laura snapped her eyelids up, aghast at herself. Words

5

heard but not comprehended lingered on the immediate air. "I'm sorry, I haven't been sleeping very much."

"Of course you haven't," said Catherine Fourte approvingly, "which bears out my point. Why don't you let Julian and Naomi take Max for a few days? They'd enjoy having him, and it might be good for both of you."

The offer had already been made, and was doubtless well meant, but to Laura there was a semi-European concentration on what was almost certainly the last male in the existing Fourte line. Julian and his wife were childless and likely to remain so, and Marianne and her Paris-based husband had so far produced four daughters. Of the most recent birth, she had said firmly from across the Atlantic, "This is it."

So, in time, Max would be trained to take over Fourte, Inc., the small, prestigious family-owned corporation, which produced in an unhurried manner custom-hand-crafted furniture. Bernard had been the head because it had been decided that Julian, with less flair and more caution, was better placed as chairman. The business with its offices and showrooms on upper Fifth Avenue had been Bernard's toy and his joy; the fact that it made money was a frill. All three of the Fourtes had been left financially independent by their mother.

Never too soon to indoctrinate a very small boy in the exquisite joining of beautiful woods, the virtues of various leathers and fabrics, the felicitous marriage of function and elegance. And it was true that, the funeral over and the house empty except for Mrs. Wedge, Laura could retreat into a private burrow.

But Max should not be exposed so soon to another upheaval, and she said a second no, polite but definite. She discovered that in her tiny interval of exhausted nonawareness people had indeed begun to trickle into the dining room—and here, chief of protocol for the day, was Mrs. Wedge with a tray which she set down on a Fourte, Inc., cocktail table, stepped for ashtrays or flowers.

"The cheese is hot, madam," she said temptingly to Laura.

So it was, on thin delicate rounds of rye with a black olive halved on top. There were also triangles of chicken and watercress sandwiches, and slender rolls of sweet pink ham toothpicked around cream cheese. All of it inedible.

"Thank you, Mrs. Wedge. Can you sit down yourself now?"

"In good time," said Mrs. Wedge majestically, and sailed away.

Was it a side effect of the sleeping pills the doctor had prescribed that made her stomach so rebellious at the sight of food? Laura had taken them obediently, even though she had a primitive fear of rendering herself unconscious, and she assumed that they had been effective even with echoes continuing to penetrate like thumbtacks poked through soft cloth.

Things she and Bernard had said to each other, and not very long ago.

Something Delahanty had said.

"You won't do anyone any good by starving yourself," said Catherine Fourte severely, picking up a cheese round.

"I know," said Laura.

Outside, it had begun to snow.

Two

Nothing lasted forever, in spite of impressions at the time, and when she had closed the front door with finality on the ash-and-white day, Laura went out to the kitchen to thank the housekeeper for her single-handed coping. "Have you heard from Irma?"

"Not since the day before yesterday." Mrs. Wedge was stout, there was no other word for it, and with her sternly up-brushed and knotted gray hair had the slightly affronted look of someone's grandmother in a very old album. "Treats herself like glass, that girl does."

Although the maid who came in by the day was her niece, she had the peculiar ability to stand back at a critical distance. Laura, who tended to agree, nevertheless felt compelled to say, "But if she's sick—"

"Nobody should have a cold this long," said Mrs. Wedge, laying it down like a dark decree. "And at such a time. If I were you, Mrs. Fourte"—the *madam* had been strictly for show—"I wouldn't give her beyond tomorrow. There are other frogs in the sea."

She glanced at the clock on a miraculously cleared counter. "If you're going to get Max up from his nap, why don't you bring him down to me and have yourself a nice hot bath and a lie-down?"

The suggestion was too alluring to refuse. Max was fond of Mrs. Wedge, who had been a part of his life far longer than his stepmother, and the prospect of being out of her suit and stretched flat on her bed made Laura a trifle light-headed with anticipation. Tomorrow there would be the dreadful little cards, ordered at once by competent Naomi, to inform the recipients that Mrs. Bernard Fourte grate-fully acknowledged . . .

But that was tomorrow. In the doorway, Laura said, "And then do you know what we should do? Turn off the phones."

Mrs. Wedge was scandalized. "Oh, Mrs. Fourte, we can't do that!"

"I don't know why not. Everybody essential has been here, or written to, and this isn't the day to listen to people selling things."

And, upstairs, Laura immediately silenced the bed-room extension. She had been so acutely scrutinized and assessed for the past four days that even a blind instrument had the appearance of a clever, hooded little spy. Then she changed into a robe and tiptoed into her stepson's room.

She had married Bernard after a traumatic event in her life whose effect she had scrupulously explained to him, but it was Max with whom she had really fallen in love. He had the charm of a woodland creature—a very small fawn?—with a deceptive air of fragility and a temper so basically sweet that his rare rages turned Laura speechless with laughter.

He was awake now in his yellow pajamas, playing ab-sorbedly with a game cased in tough plastic in which the trick was to maneuver two tiny bright steel balls into place to provide eyes for a mouse in a bonnet. His bent head was light brown, his skin had the milkiness bequeathed to him by the girl who had hang-glided to her death on a visit to Arizona when he was only a few months old.

Only his eyes, raised at the opening of the door, were Bernard's; a vivid, almost burning gray which Laura had never encountered before. She said, "*Here* you are" as if she had been combing the house unsuccessfully for him because his life must be kept as usual as possible at this time, and Max beamed crookedly at her, hoisted himself upright in his crib, and held up his arms to be lifted.

"Aura," he said welcomingly.

There had been a discussion at the outset as to what he should call her. Laura had ruled out *Mama*, as in time he would have to know that she had not given birth to him, and the coy, all-purpose *Mimi*. She had said to Bernard, "I do have a name. Why can't he just use that?" and when it came out *Aura*, Bernard had said with an appreciative glance at her, "You know, that's not bad."

She picked him up, held him tightly against her, and plopped him back, letting down the side of the crib. "We have to get you dressed, Mrs. Wedge is looking for you."

"Edge," said Max contentedly, allowing himself to be divested of his pajamas.

He was going to be a slow talker, which had concerned Bernard to the point where Laura had taken him for a thorough examination. Barring a dysfunction, which did not exist here, said the pediatrician, talking was very much like walking; some babies did it earlier than others and by age five all were at the same plateau.

Presently Laura turned him over, arrayed in navy-and-white jersey and blue corduroy overalls, to the housekeeper. When she went back upstairs, she did not take the hot bath recommended. Just now, that would be an invitation for another death to come seeping drowsily back.

Her father's, in London, on a trip partly to see his publisher and partly to gather background for a new book. Robert Gillespie had a discerning eye and an uncanny ear, but his fingers grew impatient with a pencil. It was Laura who filled notebooks with the weather, which numbered buses went where, the ease with which one could get befuddled on the underground at Earl's Court, the dates of flower shows, the time it took to walk across St. James's Park.

It was Laura, too, who after lunch at the Audley had cried, "Look out!" at the terrible, impossible pavement-mount of a front grill and wheels—a panicked driver in a car which later proved to have had a snapped tie-rod—and dodged to safety while her father was irremediably crushed.

They were separated by only a few feet. If she had run the other way, tried to propel him out of sheer strength—

Time and a therapist taught her that in that case they would both have been killed. Still, there were crop-up moments when she had said sadly and illogically to herself, "*He* would have saved *me.*"

Not even the most wishful Freudian could have taken Bernard Fourte for a father figure except to his young son. When he asked her to marry him, Laura said, somehow obligated to do so, "You are keeping in mind that you'll be getting a female who was a trifle mixed up?"

"But I am neither," said Bernard, gray eyes smoky, and kissed her.

* * *

11

As if to fool her body into obeying her at this unlikely hour, Laura undressed, put on a nightgown, pulled the curtains over the white spin at the windows, and got under her covers.

Even though she curled on her side away from it, the other bed was not a reproach, even at night. How many times had her reading lamp gone out on its emptiness until Bernard came home, considerately quiet, to occupy it?

"A buyer and a lot of technical talk, you'd be bored," he had said when it began, six months into their marriage. Or: "An old customer, ninety I should say, who tells the same anecdote every fifteen minutes between cigars." The furniture house would make some intrusions, inevitably, but he wanted to keep them at bay as long as possible.

Laura believed him because, practically speaking, he gave her no reason not to. It was as impossible to pinpoint the exact time when she knew otherwise as to observe with the naked eye the unfolding of a bud.

This was the true and functioning double standard; she had been expected to accept those excuses as the euphemisms they were. As Bernard's wife and the preceptress of his son, home was a seemly place for her to be, happy when he wanted her and philosophical when he didn't. Laura could not doubt that he was fond of her, but as a man who could not reasonably be expected to eat the same dishes all the time, his had to be a varied diet.

That was a thought to send a shiver down the back of her throat, and it was something she could never ask him. But, granted that it wasn't true, that his evening companions were always women, it was a situation unendurable to Laura even for Max's sake and for the minimum four years before he would be able to understand why he was being abandoned for a second time.

She told Bernard so. He assured her seriously that she was entirely wrong and, somewhere, dug up a tottering man in a cloud of cigar smoke with whom they both spent an interminable evening. Even in her wrath, Laura could see the funny side of it—and there was a real danger right there, that somehow Bernard would coax her into becoming a condoning partner.

The notion steeled her. The next week, when he came into the bedroom, careful as usual not to wake her, she said into the dark, "Bernard, I'm sorry for all our sakes, but this is not going to work."

He snapped on the light. "First, Delahanty, and now you." There was a red graze on his cheekbone. "I should never have let him deputize for me that day he took you to lunch."

In her amazement, Laura forgot her instant color and in fact what she had intended to follow up with. "Delahanty *hit* you?"

Bernard took off his tie. "He did indeed. One gathers that Irish eyes are not always smiling."

"So you've lost your designer."

"No." It was rueful, as Bernard sat on the edge of his bed and busied himself with his shoelaces. "He's too good. If he shows up tomorrow with an apology . . ."

Laura suspected there was small chance of that if the extremely civilized Delahanty had felt strongly enough to resort to violence. She said, countering what had been a counterattack, "How do I come into it?" but Bernard had simply shaken his head, indicating an imperative need to get his abused cheek under a hot shower, and disappeared.

Because of his instant absorption in sketches brought to the house one weekend, he could not have seen the searching curiosity of Delahanty's gaze on Laura when he was first introduced to her, or that homing, wordless blue on other occasions, or heard his voice at the lunch when, having retrieved her napkin for her, their fingers brushing, he had said, "You may want to hack my head off for this, but how did you become Mrs. Bernard Fourte?"

The proper and aloof thing to say to that was "In the usual way." Instead, after returning his contemplation for a blind few seconds, Laura said, "I think I'll have the grilled sole."

Pouring rain. In the taxi going back to Fourte, Inc., she asked out of a number of elisions, "Why do you work for him?"

"Because he gives me my head. My aforementioned head." Delahanty stared through the clicking windshield wipers, said with deliberation, "I am going to do this," and took Laura's hand and turned her gently toward him.

This meeting of mouths was very different, not confident but questing and then delighted. When it was over, Laura said shakenly, "Well, that's that."

Delahanty, understanding her perfectly—she would not be a feminine Bernard—said nothing.

And, not very much later, Bernard ceased to exist.

Laura woke to full darkness with the initial puzzlement of someone not normally a daytime sleeper. Something healing had happened in the intervening hours; for the first time since finding the police car in the driveway she was ravenously hungry.

14

There were stray lamps on in the empty living room. The kitchen was a summing-up of warmth and normality, with Max having a repast of cocoa and soft-boiled eggs on toast, cut up for him by Mrs. Wedge. The clock said six.

Instantly, because of its very difference from the post-funeral delicacies, it was the innocent kind of food which Laura's stomach wanted. To the housekeeper, who had started to rise, she said, "No, stay where you are, I have to move around," and put cold water in a pan and added two eggs.

"Mr. Delahanty called," said Mrs. Wedge.

"Oh?" Butter out, two slices of thin brown bread placed in the toaster with a steady hand for pressing down when the time came. "What did he want?"

"He asked how you were. I told him you were resting."

"Which you will have to do too, Mrs. Wedge, but you must have a glass of sherry with me first."

Mrs. Wedge, who had been in the Fourte employment from Bernard's prep-school days, allowed pleasedly that she wouldn't mind. A cup of junket, his favorite dessert, was produced for Max. For the near end of such a ravaging day the big pleasant room was extraordinarily tranquil, snow sitting jealously on the windowsills but unable to get in.

Max uttered no electrifying shriek. That was yet to come.

Three

A number of people whose names Laura didn't recognize had paid final respects to Bernard, and some of the flowers had come to the house. She kept the ones that did not seem haloed around with hushed organ music; the others, including a few costly tributes which significantly carried no cards, she had delivered to the local hospital.

At eight o'clock, white roses under a mirror between two windows and purple-touched white tulips on an end table were like exclamations of silence in the spacious living room, copper and soft ivory and blued gray with tart little bites of lemon and marmalade here and there. Laura had long since bathed Max and tucked him into his crib. Mrs. Wedge, up since daybreak, had needed no urging to retire to her own bed.

On the table that held the tulips, the telephone rang, and a single snowy petal fell off in surprise.

"Bissis Fourte?" It was Irma, voice so distorted with cold that she might almost have been pinching her nostrils with the fingers not occupied with the receiver.

There followed a long string of apologetic symptoms and, as if to fend off any sensible suggestions, a further string of measures she had already tried. At nineteen, Irma was close to unstoppable when she had the bit firmly in her teeth.

Laura ceased listening in any real sense a few seconds into this volley, and only said an absent, "That's too bad," when a heavily breathing silence told her that the girl was expecting something. It struck her belatedly that under the altered circumstances she would not need Irma or any replacement; it would be ridiculous for her able-bodied self and a small child to have two people taking care of them.

She was too tired to explain all that now, and in any case Mrs. Wedge had to be consulted for reasons of policy even though the addition of a full-time maid had not been her idea but Bernard's. Laura said, "Yes, I understand," to Irma's trump card, the fact that she would feel just awful if she infected Max, and was able to hang up.

Immediately, containing in its opening half ring someone's frustrated dialing efforts, the telephone sounded again.

Laura waited seconds before she answered it. Should she, after that first late afternoon, have taken a miniature screwdriver to the instrument's bottom plate, just to see if anything tiny and alien nestled inside? But, not being given to the disassembling of phones, she would scarcely recognize anything tiny and alien.

"Hello?"

"Laura." Once heard, Naomi Fourte seldom had to identify herself; her voice had a timbre that wasn't far off a man's. "We've been anxious about how you survived the day, and decided to give you a call."

And also curious to see if, funeral over and guests departed, the police apparently satisfied that Bernard's murder was one more example of the senseless violence which seemed to proliferate daily, the line would be relaxedly in use? Irma couldn't have maundered on for above five minutes, but to an impatiently sweeping finger just catching up with the busy signal that might have been the last five minutes of, say, half an hour.

Although, for all the X-ray attention lavished on her for the past few days, Laura was reasonably sure that Bernard had not told his brother and sister-in-law about her intention of a legal separation until the details of the divorce he would certainly and ultimately want could be worked out. The fact that he had done nothing about the will made at the time of their marriage would indicate that.

"I had a nap this afternoon, but I'm still not going to stay up much longer," said Laura to Naomi. She added casually, "Tomorrow may be a little hectic. Mrs. Wedge's niece has just been on the phone to say that her cold will keep her away for a few more days. How are you and Julian?"

"Oh, you know . . ." Face to face, that would have been accompanied by a dismissive, it's-too-grim-to-even-talk-about flip of the hand. Although the name somehow suggested otherwise, Naomi was as fair as the Fourtes, with a gaunt, critical elegance and the fast-snapping eyelashes which warned of a short attention span.

(She had been critical on the subject of Laura's hair, which could pass for black until sun or lamp light caught winks of ruddy bronze in the feathered curves against cheeks and nape. "Why do you throw those interesting bones away? If you let it grow you could wear it drawn back." Like hers, she meant. "I don't think so," Laura had answered with amiability, and that was the end of it.)

"Incidentally"—it wasn't incidental, Laura knew intuitively; it was the whole point of this communication— "we've had the strangest call from Homer Poe. Everybody knows what a prophet of doom he is, of course, but according to him Bernard felt threatened for days before it happened."

Delahanty.

Whom Laura had known she must avoid, after the intoxicating contact in the taxi, because to do otherwise would be to create an emotional shambles. But there was no way out of the follow-up occasion, the details of which had caused Bernard to request a surrogate lunch partner for her: the in-house cocktail party to mark the seventy-fifth anniversary of Fourte, Inc.

As well as staff, a few selected customers were on hand, and they wanted to meet the head designer. Delahanty, who had delivered not an apology but his plans for departing elsewhere, was there as a civility in the case of a pre-planned event; tall, immaculate, a trifle grim.

At an unrememberable point when Bernard had conducted her into his office, Laura had heard him answer his phone with a brief, accustomed "Delahanty." Finding him beside her at a window overlooking the park, she said as a reining-in of all her senses, "You must have had a christening. Few babies escape it."

"Thomas, sometimes called Tom." He was apparently trying to commit her eyes to memory. "And you are Laura, sometimes called . . ."

The bite of imaginary endearments murmured by Bernard in the dark under coverlets caught up with him in the clenched line of his long cheek. "I'm finding that I can't stand this," he said simply, and moved away.

"If Homer knows something which I certainly didn't, he should go to the police at once," said Laura into the telephone. And if the white tulip which had shed a petal at the sound which heralded Irma's call, why didn't it disintegrate completely now? "I hope you told him so."

A tension which had pulsed up over fifty miles went flat. "I think he's just trying to keep a foot in the door," said Naomi. As with many of her utterances, this had an air of cruel accuracy. "If you change your mind about letting us have Max for a few days, give us a call, will you?"

Good-nights were exchanged—and, thought Laura, putting the receiver back, Naomi had not answered her.

Out of circumstances which nobody could fathom, Homer Poe had been a close friend of Bernard's father, and became an inevitable part of the Fourte inheritance. He admitted to a patently false sixty-five, and resembled a bereaved frog. Divorced by two wives, he spent a good deal of his time on the telephone to his stockbroker, giving instructions rather than receiving advice. For the rest, he went about plunging whole households into gloom.

Inflation. The gnawing away at the country's midsection as if heartworms were at work. The Middle East. His friends the Carews were turning into a pair of alcoholics, and so, if you asked him, were the Holmans, she if anything worse than he. (This alone should have told him something, but it did not.) A man he knew had put on just your kind of roof, and in less than a year it had come crashing through, mangling an infant in a crib.

Was it sheer need to deflect his terrible litanies that made people confide in Homer? Bernard had obviously told him about the scuffle with Delahanty, but it was odd that he should have chosen that particular diversion.

No man could relish being marked, however slightly, by a male fist in his own employ. The incident couldn't have been surprised out of Bernard by a direct question; he was far too agile-witted for that, and besides, by means of hot water and medicated cream applied frequently during the night, he had reduced the graze to the point that in the morning, a touch of Laura's pancake concealed it completely.

So, for reasons of his own, he had wanted it known that Delahanty had landed at least one blow.

It did not take a close follower of the stock market to be aware that the past week had contained some record drops. All of Homer's waking concentration would have been for his portfolio, so that not until today had he gotten around to airing his piece of information. And, to judge from the caution of his wording to Naomi and Julian, been warned by the Fourte lawyer about the inadvisability of making what amounted to an accusation at this late date.

Laura doubted that Homer would have gone to the police in any case. He liked dire things to happen—disaster spruced him up like vitamins—but not in any way that involved him directly. He was relying on the Fourtes to do his work for him. If any analogy connected with childhood had not been so grotesque, Laura would have thought him like a boy planting unpleasant things on doorsteps, ringing bells, ducking around corners to see what would happen.

And what, indeed, would happen?

To the onlookers, Laura had today been ringed firmly around by the solid protection of the Fourtes. After eight months among them, she knew otherwise; the protection was for the family name and ultimately for Max. They wanted no shabby gossip-column paragraphs about Bernard's actual manner of life, but if there was a single string that provided a hold, they would move in their own way,

21

powered by money and influence. And nobody would know about it until it was too late.

They could not be ignorant of Bernard's nature. They had relied rightly on Laura's pride to keep her from saying to the police, "I'm afraid you have a wide range of suspects. Angry husbands, jealous women, and, for all I know, a few angry wives . . ."

But pride wasn't all of it. If she had hated Bernard, and wanted to hold up for public view the urbane president of Fourte, Inc., who was almost single-handedly responsible for the children's wing of the hospital—

But she had never been able to bring herself to hate him; she had only determined to take herself permanently out of the life of a man who would nibble away at her basic integrity until it was all gone and she was simply a nicely gotten-together shell known as Mrs. Bernard Fourte.

And also as "Aura." When the first shock and a certain real grief had passed, Laura had thought: Let the police find out for themselves, as they no doubt will.

She had not been entirely lucid at the time, and it had passed her by that this decision could be regarded as peculiar and highly suggestive. She was in effect removing from herself one of the most traditional of all motives for murder.

But, to date and at least to her knowledge, the police had not found out.

Analyzed, it wasn't the impossibility it seemed. Bernard had been a man of discretion—none of his affairs would be conducted anywhere near his own or other familiar doorsteps—and also of essential privacy, for all his cordial welcoming of guests. The police would have talked to the housekeeper first, under the pretext of giving Laura time to collect herself and in order for guidance in the coming interview, and received no pleasurable morsels for their pains. Mrs. Wedge had an almost feudal loyalty, and would have said, giving them her album look, that the Fourtes were as happy and devoted a couple as you could find. And why not, married only eight months, still practically on their honeymoon?

Laura's restless walking had been taking her from one end of the long room to the other; up to the white roses, where she pushed aside folds of heavy copper silk to see if it was still snowing (it wasn't); past the fieldstone fireplace centered in a horizontal wall; down again to the oak front door, from where it was possible to see a portion of the stairs in the dining room. Here she paused, vaguely puzzled.

The house was casement-windowed throughout, and the sills on either side of the door were as deep as window seats, precluding any necessity for end tables in the area which was on the way to Bernard's study on the far side of the living room.

The sill to the right upon entering was the unfailing repository for mail. Yesterday's having been glanced at and put on Bernard's desk for coping with later, it was bare of anything but ashtray and pewter-based lamp. On this particular day, no one had remembered the box at the foot of the driveway.

At once, because it was too early for bed and to settle down with a book was impossible, the mailbox became as beckoning to Laura as if it held some treasure which might be removed at any moment. She got boots and a coat from the closet on the near side of the fireplace, and a flashlight, putting her hand on it unerringly, from an end drawer of the buffet in the dining room. Immaculate order was all very well, but a part of her insisted on a personal hodgepodge place and this one was respected as such by Mrs. Wedge.

The storm had passed. She let herself out into a white night, quarter moon and a vivid strewing of stars lighting the snow which had frozen and crunched like eggshells underfoot, exhaling an icy sweetness. Not for the first time, Laura wondered how, barring invalidism, people could exile themselves willingly to climates whose year was one long flowery season.

The house behind her at the top of the long gentle hill, white-shuttered pink brick when it was not blanched to two shades of pallor, had because of its classic lines a deceptive air of great age in its protective nestle of hickory trees. It had in fact been built in the early 1920s for an artist, which was why Bernard's study, two stories high, had its huge north window.

Bernard, who with his brother and sister had grown up in a New York town house, had acquired it at the time of his first marriage. "If you don't like it, we'll find another place," he had said when Laura saw it for the first time, "but there are no ghosts, I promise you. Of any kind."

Bernard, murdered along this road in a late-afternoon mist four days ago.

Instinctively, Laura switched off the come-and-get-me flashlight with which she had been guiding herself through the belt of darkness where the driveway bisected the apple orchard bordering the road. She collected the contents of the mailbox in something approaching a scrabble, and did not dare run back up the hill; that seemed come-and-get-

24

me too. Still, she was breathless when, snow stamped off her boots, she closed and locked the front door.

Catalogues, in late December mercifully thinning out. A letter which she put aside as if she had touched an electrical current even though its sure, dark spiking had never inscribed her name before. Notes of condolence. An invitation addressed to Mr. and Mrs. Bernard Fourte—that would continue for some time—which she opened and stared at in disbelief.

There was a new mortuary in Burnbrook, and it was having an open house to which they would be cordially welcomed. A cooler head had supplied the afterthought in the lower left-hand corner: Lewis & Sons apologized if this were being received at a time of illness in the family.

Open house. Would there be refreshments? If so, would anyone dare touch them?

Laura switched on the light in the study, added the condolences to yesterday's, which she had read and would answer tomorrow, and dropped the catalogues into the wastebasket. Then she went back into the living room and opened Delahanty's letter.

Four

"Dear Mrs. Fourte: I'm sorry to intrude such a matter at such a time . . ."

It was as crisp and correct as if a pair of hostile eyes had been reading over Laura's shoulder; there was no faintest trace of Delahanty himself in it at all. The gist was that the rocking horse commissioned by Bernard as a Christmas present for his son had been delivered to Delahanty's new office by the Fourte workshop, and he would appreciate it if Laura could come and approve it before arrangements were made for crating and delivery. There were one or two departures from his original specifications . . .

He was, with renewed apologies for this inconvenience, sincerely hers, T. Delahanty.

What it all boiled down to was: I need to talk to you but I don't trust the telephone.

Laura had forgotten all about the rocking horse and, except for a jolted sensation when festive cards arrived from people who hadn't heard, Christmas itself. Fourte did not make nursery furniture, apart from an occasional copy of an heirloom cradle for a favored customer, but when Bernard had conceived the notion he had been too stubborn to go to the store traditional for such items. Delahanty's sketch, tendered after a two-week immersion in the world of horses, had so captivated him that it hung, framed, on a wall of the study.

A tight and inner coil of which Laura had been unaware relaxed and informed her that it was now time for bed. She darkened living room and dining room and went upstairs, making up her mind as if to the accomplishing of some bold brave thing that she would not take a sleeping pill tonight; that time was past.

In the light that filtered into his room from the hall, Max slept neatly on his side, small face peaceful and untroubled. Laura extracted him from under the covers with great gentleness; it was sometimes possible to bear him off for the necessary bathroom ritual and return him to his crib without waking him completely.

But not in this instance. To her light and by now experienced touch, he had at least a degree of fever, and when she left him still perched, mission accomplished, and came back with a half aspirin in the obligatory swallow of jam, his eyes lost their heavy-lashed drowsiness and took on the electrified roundness of an owl's.

Knowing better, unable to help herself even in the utter silence of the securely locked house, Laura snapped her head around. No horrifying stranger stood there, watching; no betraying shadow flicked itself out of sight. Still, what had she expected? If babies were capable of the astonishing absorption now believed in the first weeks of life, what had a two-year-old made of the new circumstances?

When she tried to lower Max into his crib again, he locked himself around her neck with such fierceness that Laura sat down with him in the armchair, cradling him against her, and talked to him in a deliberately drifty voice. She told him that tomorrow he could go out and play in the snow—would he like that?—and that when she was little she had had a cat named Snowball and she could never find him in the winter. Presently, without protest, he was under his covers again, his closed eyelids trusting, his breathing quiet.

She took the sleeping pill after all.

". . . and I wondered," said Laura to Mrs. Wedge in the morning, having told her about Irma's call of the evening before, "how you'd feel about getting along without her or anybody else? There won't be the entertaining and I can take care of my room and Max's."

An odd expression had vanished from the housekeeper's doughty face. "As to that, except for the heavy cleaning now and again, I hope I can manage as I was always used to doing, Mrs. Fourte. Blood may be stronger than water, but Irma has no business coddling herself at a time like this and I'm sure I'd be happy to tell her that we can do very nicely without her."

And indeed Mrs. Wedge had a grimly anticipatory look. Laura said hastily that she would do it, used the kitchen pad to make a note of the telephone number, and then, because his temperature was normal and for some time he had been twitching at her skirt and saying, "Out, Aura," bundled Max into his snowsuit and boots.

Although it was literally the first snow he had set foot in, and he delighted in falling down in it and pasting himself with clingy white, Laura allowed him only fifteen minutes before she brought him back in and deposited him in the playpen she had set up in the study. He had had some mild ailment, if only the reaction of the body to uncomprehended loss, and the box of acknowledgment cards awaited.

But first, Irma. After those eerie seconds last night Laura had a question to ask her.

A female voice, not the maid's, answered. No, Irma wasn't there, she had left for the doctor's a few minutes ago.

Had both she and Mrs. Wedge been wronging the girl? It was close to ten o'clock. Laura said that she would try again at eleven, and left her name. "If Irma comes back before then, would you ask her to call me?"

And so, surrounded by the tray of florist's cards and telegrams, the address book and the directory, on to the sealing-up of the engraved message.

Communications requiring a personal note having been sequestered in another tray, Laura wrote envelopes and attached stamps, contriving to sever herself from the inwardness of the task as if she were a secretary. It helped, in a sense, to realize that at least some of these people were doing some hard speculating about her.

In his playpen, which he was on the whole very good about, Max worked industriously at putting together a nest of boxes so designed that when the last one went in there was a loud squeak which made him chortle with pleasure and tear his handiwork apart and start all over again. The telephone rang at intervals and was nipped off smartly by Mrs. Wedge, who had volunteered to put off anyone who wasn't urgent.

As familiar with this household as she was, she would have an accurate gauge as to urgency—and now she was in the doorway, looking baffled. "There's a Mr. Newell on the phone, something about a horse."

Laura's heart checked briefly. "I think I know what it is," she said, and lifted the receiver on the desk.

"Mrs. Fourte? This is Toby Newell." It was a briskly

29

amiable voice. "You don't know me, but I have a rocking horse in my office that my secretary has almost broken her toe on for the fourth time in three days. Would it be possible for you to come in today and give it a smart slap on the rump?"

"I'm sorry, yes, I'll get the two o'clock train. You're at—?"

She verified the address Delahanty had written, and was told, "Right. I think you'll like the horse. If my legs were a little shorter, I'd take a jaunt on it myself."

Sensibly, no hollow words about her bereavement, although Delahanty must have told him why there was such an object parked in his office. Laura said good-bye and hung up. The two o'clock train from Burnbrook, decided upon just before her sleeping pill took effect, seemed exactly right; there was no suggestion in it of lunch or anything else.

"Mrs. Fourte?" It was Mrs. Wedge again, but this time she closed the door of the study behind her. "There's a woman here, she didn't give her name. I told her you were busy but she said she'd wait. I really don't know what to do with her."

It wasn't the words but the high unaccustomed flush on the housekeeper's cheeks that gave Laura some idea of what to expect. With her bedroom window looking down over the driveway that circled around the back of the house to the garage, of course Mrs. Wedge knew about Bernard's frequent small-hours arrivals.

"I'll see her," said Laura, and stood up, arching her back against the long interval of immobility.

It was perhaps shocking that as she started for the living room she felt only a mild curiosity: What can they be like? There would be an answering speculation in the living room, but all she could do was shape her hair swiftly into place before she walked through the doorway and into confrontation—it was instantly that—with the woman strolling about as if in a gallery where she might or might not buy something.

She was older than Laura by several years, and as mannered as a portrait. Her honey-colored hair was ruffled artfully across her brow, almost to the depth of eyes that matched, and even in a straight Persian-lamb coat over tapered black trousers, she had the kind of sumptuousness that makes a mockery of tense and cross-grained dieters. She looked to Laura as dangerous as broken glass.

She said, unhurriedly putting down a piece of crystal which she had been inspecting for credentials, "I can't imagine that you want introductions, but your husband was a friend of mine. I felt I had to come even though I stayed away from the funeral yesterday."

"Oh?" said Laura. It was, in civil intercourse, almost the most terrible word she knew.

"To see—" a hand came up to linger over the smoothing of a half-hidden eyebrow arch "—what you were like, I suppose."

"And now you have," said Laura, who had propped an elbow against the mantel, "and yes, I do notice your ring." She extended her own long-fingered left hand to exhibit the star sapphire which Bernard had given her upon their engagement and the apparent twin of which was being brought to her attention. "They're very pretty, aren't they?"

This was not the desired reaction; she ought to have changed color or backed instinctively away, as she might well have months ago when she was still in her contented ignorance. She said, "If that's all, I have things to do and no doubt you have too," and moved decisively away from the mantel.

"I would have gone quietly," said the woman. If a voice could be accorded a glitter, hers had one. She came a step closer on a waft of unidentifiable scent; it might have been the atmosphere in the room which suggested spoiled perfume. "You didn't have to *kill* him."

And there it was, in words at last; in the case of slain and unfaithful spouses, there wasn't usually far to look.

Laura walked past her visitor into the dining room, called ringingly, "Mrs. Wedge?" returned, said, "Excuse me," went into the study, and came back with Max balanced on her hip. She said to the housekeeper, who had materialized, "If anyone phones in the next hour or two, would you take a message?" and mounted the stairs without a backward glance.

It would have been cruel to leave a lesser personality in charge of that venom wrapped in Persian lamb, but even before she reached the upper landing Laura heard the front door close. Because of its weight, it was impossible to slam.

So, although Bernard's tastes had seemed to incline toward the understated in all areas, he had really preferred opulence in at least one. Of course, to be fair, that was only a single sample. Perhaps the others were not as bloomily, goldenly ripe.

Had the hang-gliding girl allowed herself to be taken by a dangerous air current without caring much for those few seconds? In the single photograph Laura had seen, she had looked quite young and gentle.

Max, who had been up for a whole hour longer than

32

Laura under the tutelage of Mrs. Wedge, did not demur about being settled for his nap. The frightened stare of last night, and the desperate clinging, might never have happened—but today his familiar room held buttercup light even with the curtains drawn, and he had not been dreaming whatever two-year-olds dream when the main prop of their universe has been removed.

At the bottom of the stairs, Laura was met by an icebox cold. Mrs. Wedge had been vacuuming, and it was her habit when she did so to open all the windows as if she were plying an energetic, dust-dispersing broom. Or, this morning, was it something more than that; a thorough ridding of that alien, unwelcome fragrance? The housekeeper would not criticize Bernard by so much as a syllable, especially now, but like most people with guarded tongues, she had her own methods of comment.

It was eleven-thirty. Irma answered on the fourth ring, still sounding clogged but with an undercurrent of importance. She had had to wait at the doctor's—"*You* know how that is, Mrs. Fourte"—and then he had given her a prescription and ordered her to bed. "And I don't know about coming back."

It was a piece of luck, sparing Laura the task of telling her that she wouldn't be needed, but there was a certain savor to the girl's phrasing and Laura thought she knew what was behind it. She said deliberately, "Is it something about your hours?"

"Oh, no, Mrs. Fourte, and Max is a perfect doll. It's just that"—Irma was usually to be observed in the close proximity of a mirror, whatever room she was in, and Laura had a vision of her now, admiring her large and somewhat vacant brown eyes and turning her swanlike neck this way and that as she spoke—"the doctor says I have very delicate nerves."

And therefore, if the doctor could really be credited with such a diagnosis, could not bear to be in the same house with a widow who might conceivably have gotten away with murder.

"I see. Well, who knows, maybe there's something he can give you for it," said Laura, crisp and dry and knowing that this was a feather delivered at a target which could only register a resounding thunk. "I'll have whatever we owe you in the mail today. In the meantime, Irma, did you tell Max what happened to his father?"

At the other end of the line there was a horrified gasp and a denial, which even to Laura's unsympathetic ear sounded genuine. "When I put him to bed with those policemen in the house, and he kept saying 'Daddy,' I just pretended not to hear him and went on talking."

A course which would present no difficulties to Irma, and the next morning she had called up to announce her cold.

Laura, attacking the other tray, wrote brief notes until one o'clock. Not the simplest of undertakings, it was complicated by a direct accusation and a sly innuendo within the space of a half hour. What had Dear Mr. and Mrs. Wharton actually said to each other when they learned of Bernard's murder? And the distant cousins whose name was Eustace and who were not mentioned in the will? "Interesting to know where his wife was at the time"?

In the kitchen, while Laura assembled a toasted sandwich of thin-sliced tomatoes and Roquefort blended with a little butter, Mrs. Wedge asked darkly about Irma. Informed, she made a sound of tart displeasure. "I'll tell you what it is, Mrs. Fourte, she's never been the same since they did some movie filming here in town three years ago and she was in a crowd scene. She came out a tiny dot, but it went to her head."

"Or her neck," suggested Laura, and Mrs. Wedge gave her a wise glance. "Exactly what I said to her at the time. 'Having a great long snaky neck like that Katharine Hepburn will never make an actress out of you.' I thought chicken pie for dinner, I'll fix Max his own little one with his name on it, and salad."

Laura said that sounded very nice and, the way thus opened, explained that she would start looking around for a reliable baby-sitter but right now she had to catch the two o'clock train to New York in aid of Max's Christmas present. She mentioned the sketch in the study, and Mrs. Wedge was far too captivated to care about baby-sitters.

"A rocking horse!" she said, pressing both hands to her imposing bosom as if unlikely memories stirred there. "Oh, my."

Burnbrook, originally an artist's colony and fishing village, still retained some of its original flavor even though its artists were now the kind whose shows drew automatic attention from public and press. Money and chic had drifted up from Manhattan along with advertising directors, television executives, well-padded surgeons, and witty psychiatrists, but although this had meant sweeping changes along the town's main street, it also ensured enough land in private and unworried hands for stretches of woods and even meadows to be safe from development.

There were two ways of approach to the station from the Fourte property.

One was the new Shore Road, fast, four lane, studded with essential, unattractive service outlets. The other, which it had largely superseded, was the Coast Road, winding, shabbily maintained, with something pleasant to be seen around every curve. Except in rare cases where speed was of the essence, it had been Bernard's customary route, and Laura used it today.

There was nothing to flinch from; no freshly wounded tree or broken guardrail or even the knowledge of blood dark under the snow. The Mercedes had contained that. The police were still holding the car, although a polite if cool-eyed detective lieutenant had told Laura that a preliminary report indicated only Bernard's fingerprints and a few of hers.

This in no way interfered with their theory, to which they apparently still clung, of a hitchhiker or another motorist in pretended distress; more people than not wore gloves in a very cold December.

"Apart from the fact that my husband would never have stopped for a hitchhiker," Laura had said, "there would have been no point in it so close to home, and the same is true of a woman driver stranded alone. Bernard would have called out to her that he'd phone a garage."

She had been given a dry glance. "It wouldn't be the first time a woman who seemed to be alone was definitely not. Your place looks like money, Mrs. Fourte, and so does the car."

Was that why they were showing no real interest in her so far, except for a few skeptical questions; because she so adamantly put obstacles in the path of a handy hypothesis?

At the station, there was no one she knew among the people patrolling the platform, and she didn't go into New York with such frequency as to be automatically familiar to the man at the ticket window. In addition, and unusual for her, she had pulled on a dippy-brimmed cream wool hat to anchor the hair still slippery from its day-before-yesterday washing.

The train pulled in. Laura settled herself at a window seat, caught a few flashing glimpses of the Sound, began, inevitably, to hear again Irma's pointed voice: "*You* know how that is, Mrs. Fourte."

Yes. On the day of Bernard's death, the day when she had driven obediently to her appointment at the Lowell Clinic because he insisted that it had taken her an inordinate length of time to recover from a virus attack and she ought to have a checkup to be on the safe side.

As the clinic had facilities for almost everything, only four of about two dozen chairs in the waiting room were vacant. Laura's appointment was for three o'clock, and she was a little early. There was no sign at the desk to warn patients to make themselves known to the receptionist; in fact, at the moment there was no one at the desk. She opened the book she had brought with her, secure in the innocent belief that against three P.M. on this particular doctor's appointment sheet was "Laura Fourte," and that in due time she would be called as other people were being called intermittently.

It became three-twenty and then three-forty. Even though Laura was here, in place, and not anxious to undertake the twelve-mile drive again very soon, this was ridiculous; medical emergencies arose, no doubt, but they should say so.

At three forty-five she approached the desk, which now had a woman seated behind it, dialing. She said, "I'm Mrs.—"

"Would you wait just a moment, please."

"I have already waited forty-five minutes. I—"

The woman held up a stern palm, consulting a note before her, and said into the telephone, "Mrs. White? Doctor wants you to have a thorough physical, including an echo-chamber test. I can set that up for you right now . . ."

The devil with the doctor, thought Laura, rebellious, and took her departure.

There was something peculiarly maddening about a mission, unwelcome to begin with, which could not be carried to completion. This was the time of semisuspension, when Laura's ultimatum to Bernard had been lost in the astonishing revelation about Delahanty; emerging from his shower, massaging cream into his cheek graze, he had said simply, "Give me until the weekend, Laura. We'll work it out."

Accordingly, as a salvaging effort on the late afternoon with a mist beginning to rise, Laura detoured to the Burnbrook Public Library; there was also the chance of new books in. The entire absence of any other car reminded her belatedly that a weekly closing at two P.M. had been shifted from Wednesday to Friday.

The lieutenant: "And you didn't know this, as a regular library-goer?"

Here was the area that mattered, from a time point of view. A wife who had made permanent plans for her husband would have made a show of keeping a doctor's appointment, as that was a matter of record, but after that? Granted that the husband was now on the train, and the course indeflectably set—

"The hours changed only last week. I should have remembered, but I didn't," said Laura.

And so arrived home from the opposite direction, to find the patrol car in the driveway.

New York's share of the storm had turned to soiled slush. Laura took a cab to the address she had memorized, and after a brief inspection in the lobby, as suddenly nervous as if she were job hunting, discovered that the floor she wanted was the fifth.

What, with the night to reflect upon it, had Julian and Naomi done about the confidence passed along to them by Homer Poe? Which might not be true. Remember that, and at the same time wipe out what Delahanty had said to her over the telephone a bare two hours after Bernard's murder had been announced.

. . . And here, casually not troubling with the initials of associations to which he might belong, was the office door of Tobias Newell, Architect. Laura turned the knob and walked in.

Five

The reception room had been designed to impress the knowledgeable and reassure the fearful, who would observe to themselves that the rug was on the thin side and their child could do better than that rough painting of a meadow. The woman behind the desk, fortyish, with glasses on a chain, had obviously been chosen for her efficiency.

"Oh, yes indeed," she said when Laura had identified herself, "I'm to bring you right in," and without knocking led the way through one of two doors in the inner wall.

This office was a corner one, big, and seemed full of angles and light. The receptionist, who evidently doubled as secretary and had left the door open, walked to some files and pulled out a middle drawer. Delahanty turned from the window, took Laura in with a somber blue gaze that shook her as if he had ignored her on the street, and said pleasantly, "Mrs. Fourte. Well," nodding at the beautiful thing which obtruded from a space between a leather couch and a tilt-topped desk, "there it is."

The horse, carved of fine pale wood and saddled in calf, had none of the traditional merry-go-round nostrils or jovial smile. The eager head was Arabian, the flowing mane undoubtedly real, and yet it was not a static reproduction of a horse. Even with rockers, it seemed possible that any sudden movement might fill the office with hoofbeats.

"It's lovely," said Laura. Her chest felt constricted.

"I think it came out well." Delahanty pressed on the saddle, which carried miniature stirrups. "There's an up-and-down movement, of course, and a slight forward one, lively but not dangerous. Your stepson is what, two?"

"Yes, he's two." Laura suspected that Toby Newell of the amiable voice had gone out to afford them this short interval together—and for what? The secretary's back was to them as, from an occasional riffle of paper, she put folders back and searched for others, but Delahanty, whose mouth Laura had known even if only once, was a careful stranger.

Well, he was a man who thoroughly liked what he did for a living, and what professional good could derive from being involved in any way with Bernard Fourte's widow?

Perhaps a doppelganger, that concept which carried such a deep primitive chill? Craftily lifelike down to the last dark eyebrow hair but with all memory having ceased to exist of having said, "One way or the other, I'll be in touch."

They were almost literally in touch now—and Delahanty, hands pocketed as if they were cold, was remarking of the fruition of his preliminary sketch and his meticulously drawn follow-up design, "As you've probably noticed, the tail color is a little off, and in fact the hair there isn't a hundred percent genuine. The supplier—"

But there were kinds of pain that did not have to be borne. "That doesn't matter in the least," said Laura rapidly, and bent her head as she opened her handbag.

Delahanty stopped her. "Your husband took care of it, Mrs. Fourte."

Your husband. Your stepson. Mrs. Fourte.

On the other side of the office there was a mutter of satisfaction from the interminable receptionist and a tiny roll of metal thunder as a file drawer went home. Laura said to Delahanty, "Thank you very much," and put on with deliberation the gloves she had taken off upon entering, so that what touched his palm when she extended her hand formally was cream pigskin.

"You ought to have it by the day after tomorrow," said Delahanty, conducting her politely to the door of the outer office. "Is there usually someone at home?"

As if he had never heard of Mrs. Wedge, whom he must have encountered on a number of occasions during his three years of association with Bernard. "Yes. Good-bye."

There were three people in the elevator going down, and, waiting in the lobby when the doors opened, a pinkly barbered man with a quiff of prematurely gray hair and an air of chipmunk brightness when his eyes met Laura's. She was tempted to say, "Thank you, Mr. Newell. It isn't your fault that it didn't work."

Out again to the cold and the slush, and not a taxi in sight. She would have liked to run all the way to the station, welcoming the icy, dirty spatter, but something seemed to impede her breathing and she settled for a furious ducking and sidestepping when pedestrian traffic blocked her passage.

Presently, she could see the clock. She could easily make the three-forty, the train on which Bernard had taken his last ride.

And now she would bring back that brief telephone interchange during which the detective had discreetly re-

read his notes, the uniformed men having gone, but she would apply a new perspective.

"Laura." Delahanty was unguarded at that point. "I was rummaging around in upstate barns all day and I heard the news on the radio while I was getting off the parkway. Are you all right?"

Only his tone removed it from the realm of a solicitous "Oh, did that hit you?" to someone whose head still rang with concussion.

"Reasonably. I think."

"You aren't alone there?"

For the moment, he would consider Max and Mrs. Wedge to be noncompanions. "No. There's a police lieutenant here and Julian and Naomi are on their way."

"Good." Pause, then: "It isn't the time to be saying this, and you'll have to forgive me, but I wish to God we were back in that—"

He didn't have to finish it. The taxi's windshield wipers clicking, the long kiss. He exhaled a breath which traveled audibly over the wire; it sounded torn. "One way or the other, I'll be in touch."

But, take a look by the illumination of hindsight. His brisk placing of himself far from the scene of Bernard's murder. His fervent wish, because it could certainly be construed as that, that they could return to a time of harmless dalliance, with Bernard still alive.

"*Laura.*"

It wasn't an echo. Delahanty had obviously found a cab where none had appeared to exist, and he had her by the wrist.

"I have a train to catch," said Laura, getting it out evenly although her lungs wanted her to be breathless.

"The devil with the train." Delahanty glared with such

ferocity at an arm-linked and chanting band of schoolchildren that they took a detour. "Do you think I *wanted* to go through with that frightful charade?"

"Then why did you?" Laura, equally fierce, could nevertheless feel the betraying melt of the wrist by which he continued to hold her captive.

"That wasn't Toby's receptionist. From the ones I've seen, he could call them all back and put on his own Follies," said Delahanty. "That was a ringer, and what's more, she wasn't there at ten-thirty this morning. Toby's girl developed stomach cramps and volunteered an aunt, an experienced part-time secretary. You saw how she clung, but you don't know that office. There isn't a spot in it without an accurate reflecting surface."

The impression of angles and light; yes. Julian and Naomi and probably old Catherine in conference, with a reservoir of past employees to draw upon. What if the altercation between Delahanty and Bernard had arisen over Laura? The rocking horse was no secret, and the Fourte workshop would have supplied the address to which it had been delivered because it was Delahanty's project and there was a slight departure from specifications.

Cross a pretty young girl's palm to listen for any communication between the Newell office and Laura, pay her generously for taking the day off, and put a trusted observer on the scene.

By not mentioning Delahanty's name last night when tacitly invited by Naomi to do so, Laura had stepped into a trap.

"The restaurant where we had lunch is Fourte stamping ground. Give that much to the kind of lawyer Julian can hire and he'd be off and running—after the taxi driver, for a start. I have a feeling," said Delahanty, grim, "that there's something very unpleasant coming up."

Did he mean Laura's losing Max—as she had known she must, ultimately; at the time of her marriage, simply because such an event seemed so unlikely, she had agreed to cede any claim to her stepson in the case of a divorce action brought by her—or something that went much deeper?

A man in a willowy chesterfield bumped violently into Laura and mumbled an over-the-shoulder apology. She said, "Why did you hit Bernard?"

Delahanty held her gaze for a few seconds and glanced away. "I don't think I'll go into that. . . . Come here a minute."

"Here" was an angle formed by a newspaper kiosk, screened for the moment by another long double file of lapel-tagged students, these of high school age; there was a youth conference somewhere. Delahanty held Laura tightly, kissed her, and said, "Get your train. . . . The rocking-horse won't fit in my car, but I know of a van I can borrow."

"Oh, better not."

"Better *so*, after that limpet in the office. The best defense— Besides, considering the source of the commission, wouldn't I be apt to see the horse into its permanent stall without scratches or gouging? But it's heavier than it looks," said Delahanty with a trace of private amusement, "and I won't come alone."

Something very unpleasant coming up. . . . It turned out in the short term to be Homer Poe, who greeted Laura on the train, placed his hat and his carefully folded cashmere topcoat on the luggage rack, and sat down uninvited to contemplate her out of his swampy greenish eyes.

"You're looking well," he said suspiciously.

He couldn't have seen her with Delahanty, not behind that unbroken stream of students. "The doctor insisted that I start getting away from the house every day for a few hours," said Laura. He hadn't, but it sounded plausible. "Apparently it was a good idea."

Poe leaned a little to examine the empty space around her feet and then tipped his white head back to consult the rack above. "Shopping?" he asked finally.

"No, some final arrangements about a present for Max."

The froggy features assumed a rudimentary smile. "Knows about Santa Claus, does he?"

"As much as he can at his age." Laura eased her paperback stealthily out of her handbag; she could not stand this all the way to Burnbrook and it seemed impossible that he did not have a financial journal concealed somewhere on his person.

Beside her, Poe fell to musing. This—the seething, silent activity of a chess player—was his second most terrible weapon. Smokers were apt to consume frenzied numbers of cigarettes when he deployed it; nonsmokers, deprived of even those tiny gestures, took refuge in smoothing their hair, rubbing their eyes, massaging imaginary soreness in hands or forearms.

What if he were suddenly to open his mouth and croak, "Nevermore?"

He didn't; he gave the slightly asthmatic wheeze that passed for tolerant amusement. "Let him keep his illusions. The Easter bunny too," he threw in generously. "He'll lose them soon enough. By the time he knows what life is all about it'll be legal for the IRS and the FBI and the CIA to come trooping down the chimney."

"Let's hope not." Laura opened her paperback with firmness. "Will you excuse me, Homer? I have to finish this, I promised to give it to someone else tonight."

Instead of craning to see what title could have such urgency, Poe turned in his seat to face her more squarely. "I have my own theory about this terrible business," he said broodingly.

Laura's heart gave a thump; he had, after all, just been in New York. "What is it?"

"A woman dressed and made up to look like you, at least in a mist and at a little distance, and a man with her. Maybe a man Bernard knew." Poe's eyes, magnified by his glasses, were like the pond water which Laura had collected as a child and let stand for a week: tenanted with things at an unpleasant stage of growth. "So Bernard stopped his car, naturally, and—" He shrugged.

"A decoy—I see. But if this man knew so much about Bernard's habits, and wanted to kill him for some reason, why run the risk of involving someone else?" Surprisingly, because of her sudden passionate dislike of the oracular presence beside her, Laura's heart had steadied. "Surely he could have found other opportunities."

"An accessory to murder has to keep pretty quiet," said Homer to the first objection, and, to the second, "Maybe yes, maybe no. Hard to catch Bernard alone or even get near him if Bernard had reason to be afraid of him."

There was a clear rebuttal to this, if Laura chose to challenge him with Delahanty's name: Bernard would never have considered retaining as designer, let alone having at a cocktail party where there was so much food and

47

drink about, a man whom he regarded as a threat to his life.

But—"I was rummaging around in upstate barns all day"—she didn't dare. She said as the train began slowing for Port Chester, "It's an idea, I suppose. Have you told the police?"

Poe put on a mysterious expression, which meant that Julian and Naomi had been the opposite of encouraging. "I'm pursuing it myself at this stage," he said grandly.

So *he* thought. If the Fourtes had had a family motto, it would have been a succinct "Leave Us Alone" while they got on with whatever it was by themselves. It was within their rights and entirely natural under the circumstances, but it also meant that they could make up the rules as they went along.

They had two ends to achieve: find out who had killed Bernard, and gain legal control of Max as soon as possible. With the fact of death assimilated a little more with every passing day, it could be argued that the second was becoming as cogent as the first. If a common denominator could be found to serve both—

Laura was not ingenuous enough to believe that where nothing existed to be proven, no danger lay. In theory, the burden of proof was on the law. In practice and along the way, damage could be inflicted on the innocent; allegations had far more color than retractions. Professional reputations had been smashed. Wrongful months in prison were not unknown.

At Port Chester, a number of male and female Christmas shoppers got off, smiting aisle passengers with unwieldy parcels and flapping bags. Before the exodus could be completed, Laura craned forward at a woman who had moved to a window seat toward the front of the car. "Excuse me, Homer, there's someone I know and I must say hello," she said hastily, and made her escape.

Know was a misleading term; it was the barest acquaintanceship. Still, the woman turned an instant smile when Laura asked, "Do you mind?" and dropped down beside her.

She had met Mrs. Dalloway—"Not *the* Mrs. Dalloway," explaining it with faint tiredness upon first introductions, because how many people must have responded waggishly, "What a coincidence, I'm Virginia Woolf"?—in the little park at the top of the road where she took Max on Irma's day off.

Even without playground facilities or, except on rare occasions, other children, the park was a place of great attraction for Max because of the wood ducks and mallards that cruised on a round pond and to whom he threw prodigal handfuls of bread. In summer, with its trees and wraparound of rhododendrons and dwarf evergreens, it was cool and quiet, with grass to fall down on, and through October it had been a deep drift of gold. There were also benches and a stone drinking fountain, and it was on one of the benches that Laura had encountered Mrs. Dalloway.

She appeared to be in her mid-forties, with cream-streaked dark silver hair in casual bangs. The skin that still had vestiges of a summer tan in December was almost unlined. She had smiled briefly at Laura and at Max, who was having to content himself with juncos, and resumed writing on a pad.

The following week, she introduced and explained herself. She had had heart surgery, and her doctor insisted on a brisk three-mile walk every day, although he grudgingly allowed her a short midway rest. "And that's when I do my

49

correspondence. Somehow it seems less of a task in the open air."

Now she said forthrightly, "I was so sorry to hear about your husband, Mrs. Fourte."

"Thank you." A little bare and bald, but it was impossible to reply, as to other commiserations, that those things happened. "How are you? Are you still walking?"

"Oh, yes, although yesterday with the snow I had to resort to exercises. Now that's something I *really* hate, staying in the same spot with all that effort."

"But you look so well . . ."

Moments later and by mutual consent, both Laura and Mrs. Dalloway opened their books. A glance in a compact mirror first showed Homer Poe busily applying blight to a rosy-cheeked boy, an apparent undergraduate who had doubtless been looking forward to Christmas break.

At the house, Max, in the delicious-smelling kitchen, was preparing to attack his individual dinner. Having had it explained to him that the fork-pricks in the piecrust spelled his name, he crowed to Laura even before she kissed him, "My pie, my pie!" and generously wobbled out a taste for her.

"It's a little early, but he just wouldn't wait," said Mrs. Wedge complacently.

"I don't blame him, it's marvelous. I hope it was a reasonably quiet afternoon."

Implicit in this, and not to be mentioned by either of them under the housekeeper's laws, was the possible return of the woman in Persian lamb or anyone remotely like her.

Yes, it had been. A woman just back from the south of

France had called, her name was over there on the kitchen pad, and so had Mrs. Julian. "I told her you were in New York seeing about the you-know-what," said Mrs. Wedge significantly.

That was a delicate touch; as if the Fourtes had needed telling. Laura spun at a little sound of anger and pain from Max, who had been adventurous with his fork and somehow managed to stab a finger with it.

"Rooned," he cried, using a word which Laura hadn't known was in his vocabulary, and she said calmly, whisking him up and carrying him to the sink for a run of cold water over the few drops of blood, "No, it isn't, Max, it'll be as good as new by the time"—she was wrapping a strip of paper toweling tightly around his finger—"I count ten."

And all was well. The pressure had stopped any oozing from what was a minor wound; Mrs. Wedge applied a Band-Aid before any bead of red could reappear; Max went contentedly back to his pie.

Still, thought Laura, making and carrying a drink into the living room, a little unsettling; a tiny indicator. For all his look of fragility, Max had never been a child for whom she had to dread the bumps and knocks inevitable at his age. From the abrupt erasure of his father from his life, he had received a hint of mortality.

Before she looked at the mail, she went upstairs and changed into flat black slippers and a dress-length robe diamonded in copper and white. Bracelet sleeved and Chinese collared, it would not look in the least bedroomy if she should be so unfortunate as to have a visitor.

It turned out to be a wise choice even though, in her wary flight from Homer Poe and his scarcely veiled

scenario of her coaxing Bernard to his death with Delahanty at her side, she had no sense whatever of another
little trap in the making.

Or of the gun being revisited, just to make sure that it
was still there in its bizarre hiding place, or of the quiet
moldering of the thin, tight leather gloves, scissored so that
they would have been of no help even if they were not
rapidly becoming a part of a compost heap.

Six

Max had an alphabet book upon which, even after a full month's possession, he doted like a miser with a casket of jewels; he would not allow it to be taken out of his room. Bathed and pajamaed, he waited expectantly for Laura to finish turning back the covers of his crib and join him in the armchair.

Fortunately for her, as this had become a nightly ritual, the book was a very pleasing production. End papers apart, it consisted, twenty-six times, of a single line of crisp black type on an otherwise snowy page, with a close-up color photograph facing it by way of illustration.

For Max, the crown of the whole business was the lobster; he was enchanted with its bold red claws and began to wriggle with anticipation long before the *L* was due. Tonight, when Laura recited, "*K* is for *kettle*," and began to turn past the burnished copper with a spiral of blue steam issuing from its spout, he said triumphantly, "Lobster!" and slapped down a small hand as if to keep his pet from escaping its parsley-garnished white dinner plate.

Laura gazed in surprise at his bent brown head, feathery after his bath, and the arc of eyelashes she could see. "And what's my name?"

"Aura," out of habit.

"No. *Lobster. Laura.*"

Max squirmed around to look up at her as if she might suddenly have acquired tiny eyes and feelers. "Laura," he repeated with an air of wonderment.

So, between morning and now, another little vestige of babyhood plucked away like a leaf from an artichoke. Laura, presently going downstairs, felt a slight unreasonable pang. Julian and Naomi, a pair of perfectionists, would never have allowed him to get away with "Aura" for so long.

Should she call Naomi back? No.

"About half an hour," said Mrs. Wedge when Laura returned her empty glass to the kitchen. Her glance strayed briefly, taking in the continued absence of the star sapphire with its deep flash, and from her old-fashioned expression she knew the reason why, although nobody would be able to pry it from her. "I thought I'd set the dining room table tonight, Mrs. Fourte."

Translated, this meant that in her view the allowable period for a tray table in the living room, the apparatus of crisis, was over. No doubt she was right. Laura said that would be fine and retreated to the mail and then the televised news.

But nothing reached her from the White House or the London desk, and gales which endangered shipping in the North Atlantic passed her by. Instead, she looked at Homer Poe's briskly proposed nightmare in the rising mist: the decoy woman, the killer beside her.

No; examine it in the terms of the reality he had meant. What had she herself been wearing that afternoon? A straight natural-color raincoat, because of the chancy sky, with a headscarf folded into the pocket for contingency use. It was the kind of classic which stubbornly survived other versions, and must have existed in half the closets in Connecticut.

And so would not stand out in a waiting room. Laura had spoken to no one there except, in final exasperation, the receptionist, and even then she had been prevented from identifying herself. There was no one to pinpoint her in the library area either.

With considerable mileage on it, the Mustang had begun to develop crotchets. Bernard knew that, and might easily have assumed in the indistinct light that a raincoated figure on just that stretch of road was his wife, having had to abandon her car somewhere nearby. No real need for a male companion; that was simply Homer Poe's general malevolence.

"Dinner, Mrs. Fourte."

Laura ate it, or some of it, at her accustomed place at the polished black walnut table, which was not by Fourte but an English antique, its chairs reupholstered in amethyst when the dining room had been stripped of its wallpaper and painted a white-paneled primrose. As if not to leave her completely alone on this first venture back to normality, Mrs. Wedge brought her a glass of chilled white wine with a coaxing, "And you really must have this, Mrs. Fourte."

Because Bernard had considered a dinner without wine to be a scratch meal, whatever the components, and ritual took its time about dying.

When Laura brought her plate out to the kitchen, she lingered in what was one of the pleasantest rooms in the house: warm, spacious, with vinyl flooring of red-brick pattern, crisp blue-and-white-striped ticking at three windows and butcher-block table and counters. No plants, in spite of the housekeeper's aspidistra appearance, because she confided that a sister-in-law of hers had once discovered the tiny black specks in her potato salad to be aphids instead of pepper.

Clear up one matter if possible. "I had to be out on Saturday, Mrs. Wedge"—to the mortuary with Julian and Naomi to do some frightful choosing, because it was unthinkable to them that she should delegate such a task, and then well beyond the outskirts of Burnbrook for the cocktail they all needed before lunch could be thought of—"and I wondered if a telephone man had been here to look at an extension?"

After twenty-five years of identification with the Fourtes, Mrs. Wedge was far too seasoned to show surprise at a question which might be regarded as odd. "Yes, the one in the study. He said Mr. Fourte had reported a lot of noise on the line." She slotted a rinsed plate into the dishwasher, a slight sternness furrowing her brow. "Didn't he fix it?"

Yes, Laura told her; she had simply been curious as to whether the trouble had cleared up by itself.

The Fourtes' doing, because at such a time an apparent service call would pass almost unnoticed? The police, because the inheriting wife could not account very satisfactorily for her whereabouts when her husband had been shot to death? Could that be legal?

There was a third possibility: that without bothering to mention it Bernard had indeed reported trouble on the study extension—with three others in the house, the company repair service would scarcely speed to the scene—and that it was perfectly innocent.

Still, it was the one which Laura would have used if she

did not want to go upstairs or be listened to attentively by the random spillage of visitors in those first days, and the desk was certainly where she would deal with correspondence.

For the time being, stay away from it.

Tonight, the living room was flowerless except for a pot of grape hyacinths which had arrived while Laura was in New York and sent out heady little charges of spring whenever an air current trembled by. It was a measure of her total removal from a once-familiar world, starting with the death of her father in London, that she had to grope for the last name of the sender, Alan Petrie, although she had been out with him a number of times.

Mrs. Wedge was a firm believer in drawn curtains after dark, for all her hardihood, and had made her precautionary rounds as usual. With lined bronze silk cloaking the windows and what sounded like a gale buffeting through the trees and around the house corners, there was no warning before the knocker fell loudly, twice.

There was a change in Lieutenant Drexel, and it was almost as palpable as the cold that roamed and rummaged down the room before Laura got the front door closed.

On the three or four occasions when they had met, he had struck her as being thoroughly professional and detached, without personal involvement in what was only another homicide. To look at, he might have come out of a blender into which every physical attribute had been poured, or been a representative of the thrilling bloc that said "No opinion" in polls on urgent national issues.

Now, as he took the chair Laura offered and explained without any particular conviction that he had happened to be out this way, he had stopped being an official cipher with an experienced view, simply because it happened so often all over the country, of how Bernard Fourte had met his death. He had the menace of an odorless gas, or a water hemlock nodding among blameless, edible look-alikes.

"We'll have the Mercedes back to you tomorrow, with all the objects that were in it in an envelope in the glove compartment." Drexel produced a cigarette and lit it. "Nothing helpful, but we didn't really expect it."

There would have to be stains on the leather interior, and Laura did not care if she never saw the Mercedes again. She waited, because this man with the silver-flecked brown hair and grayish-bluish eyes and the lines and crinkles of approximately forty had not come to see her about the routine return of a car.

"As I told you," Drexel moved the hand that held the cigarette in a gesture which might have been apology, "the receptionist at the clinic couldn't say whether you were there or not on Friday afternoon. She didn't recognize you from the picture in this morning's paper, but that's not too surprising, the way they come out."

The photographer at the cemetery. Laura hadn't seen the local newspaper, and had no idea of what she had looked like in that second of startlement.

"But," said Drexel, "thanks to a call late this afternoon, we do have an anonymous witness who places you at the library at about the time your husband was killed."

Instantly, Laura was back on that scene with its threat of early dusk: the old brick building unlit, the curb untenanted although there was usually bumper-to-bumper parking. Still, how tempting, because she had been there, a good three miles from the murder spot, to say that now she thought about it there had been a car . . .

And how perilous, because this was a trick. "I don't see how that can be," said Laura steadily. She had a sudden flashing vision of that honey-colored richness wrapped around in Persian lamb—walked away from, in effect dismissed, left in the charge of the housekeeper. "There wasn't another soul around. It isn't as if I had parked, or tried the doors."

"Odd, then," said Drexel. His eyes had narrowed a little as if he were considering something, and to Laura's disadvantage. Well, collusion, of course. An S.O.S. to a trusted friend: Would you be an angel and bear me out? I'll tell you what I was wearing—

"Not if someone wants to destroy my credibility. Tell me, Lieutenant, do you pay much attention to anonymous telephone calls?"

"Oh, yes. We get a lot of information that way, a good deal of it accurate, and people have their reasons," said Drexel with surprising tolerance. "They're driving with suspended licenses, or they don't want to get hauled in to testify because they have trips planned. . . . Who do you think wants to destroy your credibility?"

By quoting her own words at her, he seemed to invest them with a certain overimportance—and, as to the woman who had said that morning, "You didn't have to *kill* him," Laura could all at once hear alarm bells going off in all directions. "Whoever killed my husband, I would imagine, or someone else who wants to make me a liar. I'm on record with you and a number of other people as saying that everybody else in Burnbrook seemed to have remembered the library's early closing except me."

"And so if you were to turn around and say yes, there had been someone close enough to identify you positively, it would look odd for you to be remembering it at this late date and you would have to come up with some kind of answering description. . . . Yes, I see," said Drexel, divesting himself of a false puzzlement.

Although it might be a biological impossibility, a pulse was beginning to beat in the pit of Laura's stomach. Her refusal of the easy answer, the hitchhiker or the stranded motorist in distress, and now her denial of any witness who could have placed her safe miles away at the time that counted, were beginning to double back on her.

The lady protesting too much. Unable to see a position of danger, and so not lifting a finger to help herself.

Drexel got to his feet. "Mr. Fourte certainly kept that car like a clean-room in a lab. I'd hate to think what could be vacuumed out of mine."

"My husband was something of a fanatic about that," said Laura, back on solid ground, "and the Mercedes was new. He wouldn't even smoke in it, or allow anybody else to."

It was true that the odor of stale tobacco permeated a car's interior, destroying the sumptuous showroom smell, but although Laura had stopped smoking before she met Bernard, she sympathized strongly with people who had not, and it had become a small bone of contention: her saying that he gave the impression of prizing his car above his guests, Bernard's suave reply to anyone he undertook to drive to, say, Alaska, would be free to indulge. "A half hour or so isn't all that long, Laura."

"We noticed the ashtray," said Drexel, hand on the doorknob. "In fact, the whole inside was so immaculate that we nearly missed the roll."

For a second Laura thought she had misheard him. "The *roll?*"

"Poppy-seed. Mr. Fourte didn't come across like a man who snatched his breakfast on the way to the train," said Drexel, not quite ironic, "so we traced it to Hansen's Bakery and they said he was a frequent customer. Not that afternoon, but once or twice a week. It must have spilled out of a bag and rolled under a seat. Well, good-night, Mrs. Fourte," and on another long shiver of windy air he was gone.

Bernard had indeed liked Hansen's poppy-seed rolls, both crisp and tender and with an *H* impressed on one quadrant, but the notion of his driving fastidiously around, unaware of this homely bit of cargo, was unexpectedly touching. It was easy to imagine Delahanty unperturbed at any odd jetsam in a vehicle he drove, but Bernard?

"I'll be going upstairs now, Mrs. Fourte." The housekeeper stood in the wide entrance to the dining room, face shadowed by a soft lamp behind her. "Would you like me to get Max up for you?"

"No, thanks, I'll take care of it in a few minutes." It was an effort not to explain who the caller had been; in the days since the murder the two adults in this house had grown indefinably closer. Almost, thought Laura, like survivors.

Or, in view of their mutual silence about the woman who had brought that sharp flush to Mrs. Wedge's cheeks, accomplices.

It was one of the fortunate nights with Max. His fifteen minutes in the snow had done him no harm; his forehead was cool to Laura's cautious touch and he was processed to the bathroom and back without the alert wake-up of spoon and aspirin.

And I will not take a sleeping pill even if it means staying up all night.

61

Laura resettled herself determinedly on the couch with her book, but although determination might be a helpful attitude to bring to an assault on calculus, it stood in the way of reading as tensed muscles stand in the way of relaxation. The room was warm and tranquil in the silent house, invulnerable to the wind. Little by little, questions began to crawl coldly out of corners.

If she told Lieutenant Drexel about the woman with the matching star sapphire, and in fact the true state of the marriage:

Why was she revealing this now, on the fifth day of the investigation?

If her husband had played around—hideous phrase, but apt enough here; Bernard was not a man to have maintained a single devoted mistress—surely she had had thoughts in the same direction? She was young and attractive, and the day when neglected wives stitched tirelessly away at tapestry was long gone.

Didn't she want her husband's murderer found—or was that why she had hampered the police with a false picture from the outset?

Irma, remembered Laura, springing desperately to her feet as if an actual web had inched across the rug and begun to mount the couch. She had promised to put the girl's few days' back pay in the mail today and then forgotten all about it.

In the study, she ruffled through the checkbook, three checks to a page, which Bernard had used for utilities and other household expenses. It was a joint account on a Burnbrook bank, but when she had made the necessary calculations and after a little reflection, Laura used one of her own checks on a New York bank instead, even though it would take longer to clear. No one had told her, and she hadn't thought to ask, whether the joint account could be used before the estate was settled, and it seemed wiser to be on the safe side.

What was Irma's last name? Coppinger. Laura wrote the check, paper-clipped it to a three-line note of explanation and farewell, started to write an envelope, and came up against a lack of any address.

Get it from Mrs. Wedge in the morning.

On the other side of the river, in the small shabby house she shared with two other girls, Irma was packing.

Seven

"All I can say," said Wendy Hilliard, watching as garments were inspected and then either discarded or folded into the suitcase on the bed, "is I hope you know what you're doing."

Her tone conveyed exactly the opposite, but this was a black evening. She had no date; she had broken one of her treasured and clawlike fingernails; because it was her turn to entertain, Mildred Baracek, the third member of the renting trio, was monopolizing the living room with her marine. To get to the kitchen you had to go through there, and although it was an understood pact that nothing "heavy"—Wendy's term—should go on, who could trust Mildred? Or Eddie, whose father was of Italian descent?

The result was that unless she wanted to retire to her tiny chilly bedroom and count her fingers and toes, Wendy was incarcerated with Irma, who, contrary to her usual practice, wasn't talking.

The tight-lipped silence was Wendy's fault. From her newly exalted position as assistant manager of the yard-goods department of the local five-and-ten, and with a lettered plastic oblong to prove it, she tended to look down on her companions, a maid and a cocktail waitress who was using the money to pay for a course in shorthand and typing. Lighthearted Mildred was untroubled by loftiness, real or imagined, but Irma was as offendable as a fifty-year-old matron and, her earlier spill of excitement having been paid little attention to, would say no more.

Only the operative words remained: *talent scout*. In pursuit of *Irma?* She had that long twisty neck, true, and large brown eyes which clever makeup might turn from a cow's to a doe's, but she was peculiarly flat in every respect and not even very bright.

And here she was, full of sealed-up adventure, preparing to leave Burnbrook and these streakily painted walls behind her. Combined with a sudden burst of giggles from the living room, it was unendurable. Wendy said with spite, "I suppose you know that *talent's* another name for something else."

Fury lent Irma an unaccustomed pithiness. "I'll take your word for it." On the other side of the bed, she thrust her face closer with a curious serpentine effect of coming within striking range. "Get out of my room," she said.

By ten o'clock, Delahanty had tracked down the suggestion of looming unpleasantness which had visited him as he stood in the station with Laura.

It arose from a meeting, with all department heads present along with a few people from the agency, on the subject of Fourte's annual institutional ad, which had for the past two decades been as unvarying as the *New Yorker's* silk hat, monocle, and butterfly. There was a shadowy glimpse of Persian rug, the faint gleam of an antique Colt revolver on a paneled wall, and, bathed in warm light which seemed to coax out the smell of costly hand-rubbed wood, a classic desk, brandy colored. The engraved visiting card at a casual slant on the desk read Fourte, Inc.

In today's edgy gun-control climate, said the account man, might something else be substituted for the Colt? What about a niche with a nice piece of pewter? Pewter, not noisy, wouldn't take away from the desk but would imply the same sense of age and tradition. Or, proposed an unfortunate copywriter, a mustache cup? Everybody slued around for an incredulous look at her.

It was decided that the Colt should stay, being museum quality, but a number of interesting things emerged in the desultory discussion that followed. The Fourte treasurer, a man who wore a muffler from November through March and drank herbal tea, turned out to spend his vacations slaughtering pheasants in South Dakota. Ever since an attempted rape on her way home from an evening French class, the art director's wife had carried a small pistol in her handbag with a pair of hair scissors as backup. "And," sighting along a pencil, "she took instruction. She can use it. Bam."

"Does she have a permit for it?"

"Are you kidding? By the time we got a permit the daisies would be tall over us."

There were other contributions, among them the fact that a couple of months earlier, at her behest, Delahanty had acquired a gun for his widowed aunt, in whose no-frills apartment building there had been two assaults in the space of a month, one of them nearly fatal. The gun was a .22.

Generally speaking, and perhaps to compensate for an eight-year interval in his life, Delahanty was a lucky man.

He had so far escaped mugging, he could find taxis when it was raining, he had never gotten stuck in a voting booth. He had a dire feeling, however, that his luck was about to run out.

His Aunt Josephine, as unlikely a sister as could have been found for his pretty and volatile mother, had been waiting impatiently by the telephone; she snatched up the receiver on the first ring and said, "Gladys, it's *much* too late for you to come over. By the time you got here it—"

Delahanty identified himself loudly and with some firmness because his aunt was growing deaf and also somewhat absent-minded.

"Oh. Hello," said Josephine McCaffrey.

Although neither the neighbors nor the court had been aware of it at the time, the McCaffreys, sharing meals and a bedroom in their dark little house in the North Bronx, had stopped speaking directly to each other two years before they took over the care of the suddenly orphaned Delahanty. His parents had had their final brilliant and enjoyable quarrel on an iced-over night in February; his father, in a more dramatic gesture than usual, rushing out at a predawn hour to slip under the wheels of a milk truck, his mother, feverish with bronchitis and pursuing him in the wrong direction clad only in nightgown, raincoat, and thin slippers, succumbing to pneumonia within the week.

The bewildered ten-year-old boy they had left behind became interpreter for daunting near strangers. "Thomas, ask your uncle"—at the other end of the grim mahogany table—"if he would like another potato."

McCaffrey continuing to address himself assiduously to his plate, "Would you like another potato, Uncle Will?"

"If it wouldn't be too much trouble for your aunt."

67

The house was full of things he mustn't touch, although he felt no temptation toward china ornaments or a stuffed owl in a frozen frenzy, and church publications which were urged on him without success. An abiding odor of camphor and furniture polish seemed to leak out into the tiny back garden, where three stunted rosebushes struggled for their lives in soot and sunlessness.

His parents' estate made college possible, and Delahanty escaped.

No one had ever told him the cause of the mortal silence, but by the time he was thirteen he had realized that no volunteer fire department could have as many meetings as his uncle's apparently did, and that on those evenings the felt hat acquired a rakish tilt.

It might have been supposed that when William McCaffrey died the floodgates would open. This was not the case. Delahanty's aunt sold the frightful little house and moved to Manhattan, and a kind of wary friendship grew up between them. Even apart from physical appearance, few people would have suspected a blood connection; they addressed each other with the economy of a pair of night watchmen.

Delahanty said now, "Have you still got your gun?"

"No. Somebody broke in while I was out and took it and your uncle's gold watch. This building is a disgrace."

It had the inevitability of ants at a picnic or rain after the car was washed, except that that particular law wasn't necessarily the only force at work here. The .22 was known about and his aunt's name and address were in his résumé somewhere in the files at Fourte, Inc. And Delahanty had an emergency key to the apartment.

"When was this?"

"A week ago yesterday. Saint Clare's telephoned that there was an accident victim asking for me, but when I got there they didn't know anything about it. I believe it was a ruse."

Somebody providing himself with eating money by culling the names of single tenants from mailboxes and then watching the building's entrance from a nearby telephone booth? Maybe. Delahanty inquired without much hope, "Did you report it to the police?"

"When I had no permit for the gun? No, thank you."

Idle chat had never been a part of their relationship. After he had hung up, Delahanty located his address book, paused in the act of reaching for the receiver, thought of the telephone company records, glanced at his watch, and went out into the night.

The address Irma shared with two other girls was 279 Lucerne Street. Laura, having written it on the envelope to which she had already attached a stamp, did not immediately leave the sunny kitchen. It had been three A.M. before she could safely turn off her light without a sleeping pill, and now, at nine, she felt as if it were her own shade which had managed to consume tomato juice, a slice of toast, and coffee.

An odd and mildly worrying little thought had occurred to her at some point of turning over from left side to right or the other way around. She had finally pinned down Eunice as being the name of Bernard's first wife, but what about the surname? Had she unwittingly sent a formal acknowledgment to Bernard's parents-in-law without a handwritten line?

There had never been anything Rebecca-like about her

situation; Mrs. Wedge had welcomed her with stately approval and an invitation to change whatever domestic routines she liked. As to Eunice herself, no embroidery, but no secrecy either. "Poor girl. A great horseback rider she was, but those gliders . . ."

"The Regis Munros," said Mrs. Wedge in answer to Laura's query. She bent with surprising agility to take a cheese grater away from Max, on his hands and knees exploring the cupboard under the stove. "Mr. Munro is an architect. He designed the snail building."

She said it in all innocence, as if it might have been the Snayle Building, and the allusion identified the faint familiar ring in Laura's brain. She was not a student of architecture, but a year ago there had been a small flurry in weekly news magazines over Regis Munro, who had left his strong and sometimes controversial imprint on a number of major cities. A convoluted civic center in—St. Louis?—had been jeered at by his peers as "the world's largest snail," with angry reprints of an editorial: "A Comment on Midwestern Progress?"

And, yes, Laura had sent an unadorned acknowledgment of flowers to an address in San Francisco, this replacing a crossed-out one in Tucson. It couldn't be helped.

There was yesterday's mail to be dealt with, and that would mean more communications to go, but Laura did not want to be under another minute's obligation to Irma of the delicate nerves. She said to Max, "Let's see what it's like outside," and layered him suitably.

In spite of partial melting, the sharply dropped temperature and whipping wind had preserved her footsteps of the night before in ice. They looked calm enough in descent, frantic and uneven going uphill. A reflection of un-

reasoning fear; Laura would be glad when they dissolved
into the greenish-brown grass already visible in patches.

Max slid where he could, anchored firmly to her hand,
and made the return journey on her hip. He was trying in a
dangerously darkling fashion to tilt the tiny steel eyes into
his plastic-cased mouse while incarcerated in his playpen
when a car purred up to the front door.

Without even having to think about it, Laura plucked
him up, moved to the window, felt the small body jerk
against her in accordance with her own horrified heartbeat.
But of course it was not Bernard, issued nonchalantly forth
from the cemetery; it was Julian, topcoated so like his
brother, fair head bent as he opened the door of their long
station wagon for his wife.

Naomi was in chic mourning: tightly cinched coat of soft
black and white tweed, swoop-brimmed hat shaped from a
single piece of black felt; for ornament, only her pale
drawn-back hair, most of it eclipsed, and an austere pair of
pearl earrings.

Intuitively, Laura put Max down before she opened the
door to them. Perhaps because of his split second of confusion, and a resultant feeling of having been tricked, he
declined any greetings and buried his face in Laura's skirt.
As he was neither a rude nor a sulky child, Laura said
lightly, "Max has had a cold," as she deposited him on the
couch, and then, "New car? I was just about to get a second
cup of coffee, will you have some?"

No, they'd had the station wagon for two months—it
was invaluable now that Julian's greenhouse was finished—
and they would love a cup of coffee.

Mrs. Wedge had also glanced out the window, switched
on the coffee maker, and was assembling a tray. Laura

assembled her wits. She said, returning to the living room, "I would have called back last night but I had a visit from the police, and then it got late."

Metal could be so ice cold or scalding hot that the fast touch of a fingertip could not determine which. The reaction in the room was just as indefinable. Then Naomi said, "Are they finally getting somewhere?" And Julian, on the couch, lifted his gray gaze from an apparent absorption in Max's mouse.

Laura shook her head. "I seem to have been seen at the library after all, and they're finished with the Mercedes."

Neither of them made even a transparent demur about her being regarded seriously as a suspect. Julian said, "I can have the car seen to for you, if you like, there's a good place in Cromwell. You haven't caught Max's cold, have you? You look a little pale."

He was kind and solicitous. So had Bernard been. Laura, who did not want any discussion about sleeping pills, said, "I stayed up late to finish a book," and Mrs. Wedge arrived with coffee.

"We're on our way into town," said Naomi presently, "and we wondered if there's anything we can do for you. What's the state of the steed Bernard commissioned?"

This was boldness indeed, but Laura was not going to be maneuvered into open war with the Fourtes just now, with Max as the spoils, and an appearance of blinkered ignorance had to give a slight edge.

"Finished and beautiful. The man whose office it's in was getting a little impatient. Delahanty was there," said Laura, casual with his name and as open in her regard as Naomi, "very punctilious about some tiny detail only the designer would notice. He's arranging for it to be delivered, so that's all taken care of."

Insensibly, Julian had taken Max's plastic-cased mouse from him and was tilting it gently this way and that, unaware of the storm brewing beside him. "What was it about Delahanty, anyway? Why did he leave Fourte? Bernard mentioned an offer from Page and Holland, but the whole business seemed a little precipitate."

Had Homer Poe really not told them all of it; was he eking out his information like a serial so as to ensure a continuing interest and welcome?

"All Bernard told me was that there had been an altercation of some kind but it might be smoothed over. Julian," said Laura, suddenly and uneasily departing from her script, "had you better—?"

Too late. In one of his rare tumultuous tempers—his mouse carelessly preempted from him by an adult when he had been working on it with growing determination—Max snatched his toy, disappeared under the table in a scramble of corduroy, and reappeared on the other side. His violent breathing could be heard in the astonished silence, but it was not nearly as loud as the crack of his head on the table edge as he got to his feet, upsetting Naomi's coffee.

He was too furious to cry, although his eyes brimmed with what must have been considerable pain. Instead, he tried ridiculously to jump on the plastic case, missed his goal, and fell down.

Laura had to avert her face fleetingly; the combination of that antic and the sober, handsome disapproval of the Fourtes, like two people who had missed the point of a joke, would have undone her otherwise. She said sooth-

73

ingly, "Max, Max," and left her chair and picked him up, cradling his head into the hollow of her shoulder so that his humiliation was thoroughly hidden.

"This is stress," pronounced Naomi, applying a napkin to polished wood. The words were forgiving, the tone was not. "I've thought all along, Laura, that he would be *far* better—"

Someone knocked at the front door.

"Shall I?" inquired Julian.

"If you would, please." Laura walked with Max to the far end of the room, the mirror between the windows there showing her the curious turn of Naomi's head as part of a uniformed policeman came into view with the opening of the door.

Inaudible words were exchanged, of which Laura caught only a mention of the Mercedes. Under cover of them she whispered to Max's scarlet and now wet countenance, "You know what you look like? You look like a *lobster*."

After a second or two his mouth corners turned unwillingly up. In the mirror, the door closed on Julian and the policeman. Laura, deeming it unwise to return Max to the couch, perched him in her chair instead and dried his cheeks with another napkin. She would not scold him for Naomi's delectation, nor apologize for him. She said only, "The station wagon is new to the premises, and I think there was a confusion of identity for him just at first."

"I see. Yes, there may have been," said Naomi, but her glance at Max was not favorable.

It was startling to Laura to realize, given the distance between the two houses, different circles of friends, and the fact that Bernard had been a healthy thirty-nine, how little Naomi and Julian actually knew of their nephew. He was there, a satisfactory male Fourte, but so were bonds at the bank, and generally speaking they were only visited at coupon-clipping time.

How would Max fare at their hands, if and when? . . . Although Bernard had believed in a stretch of European schooling at the proper time, he had not wanted his son brought up abroad, and with Marianne and her husband likely to remain in Paris, Julian and Naomi had been chosen as contingency guardians until Max reached his majority.

And in fact, in case of Bernard's untimely death, Julian and a bank were custodians of the trust set up for Max when he was a few weeks old. "You don't want to be bothered with that," Bernard had said matter-of-factly to Laura.

Julian came back, dangling car keys from an oblong of leather as Naomi collected gloves and handbag with an air of wishing to be away from this troubled place. "I put the Mercedes in the garage." He paused, considering, in the act of handing the keys to Laura. "If we're not late coming home"—querying glance at his wife, who was known to dislike and avoid after-dark driving—"I could pick it up this afternoon and get it out of your way."

And possibly run smack into? . . . Laura said, "I didn't intend to visit this on you right away, Julian. Any time would be—"

"Let's see how it goes." Julian got into his topcoat with a reminding ease and elegance. "Tell you what, if you should be out, or in the tub, or busy with this young fellow, why don't you leave the keys on the mantel?"

* * *

75

Please, *please* don't let either of them encounter Delahanty stubbornly delivering the rocking horse, with a second kiss printed electrically on the air.

Some prayers were answered, others were not. This one fell in the second category.

Eight

At a quarter of four on the approach to the shortest day of the year, the park was one-quarter bitter-lemon light, three-quarters glacial shadow beginning to breed a tinge of blue. Snow still lay among the roots of the hickory trees and under the evergreens and rhododendrons that lined the iron railings on the inside, but someone had cleared a bench and Laura sat down on it while Max went for a hopeful inspection of the frozen pond.

She had succumbed to his urgent pleadings partly to escape from Homer Poe, arriving with a Christmas present for him but somehow bringing along a suggestion of doom. Laura, upstairs, had first learned of his presence when his voice rose from below: "Bad news coming for the dollar in about five years, Mrs. Wedge, but at least you and I won't be around to worry about it."

How had so many people stood him for so long? The answer that Laura suspected wasn't particularly admirable. In among his dirges, like wayward lilts, were pieces of advice about the stock market which, according to Bernard, usually turned out to be extremely valuable.

He had to be asked to sit down, and he did, and proceeded to muse, his gaze shooting away when Laura met it. She wished she had something to knit, like a slipcover for the driveway, and was finally driven to saying, "I had a visit yesterday from a woman who said she knew Bernard, although she didn't give her name."

"Is that so?" Poe was alert, although all he did was extract a cork-tipped cigarette and produce a lighter; Laura had his full attention.

"Mid-thirties, I'd guess, very well made up, goldish hair, about my height. She was wearing a Persian lamb coat."

Poe meditated on her words, or on something, seeking further enlightenment from a corner of the living room ceiling. Seconds built up into the full minute of which only he was capable. "From your description," he said at last, and immediately it became hit-or-miss, not really reliable, "it could be a Mrs. Cleef, or Creef. I'm under the impression that she was a supplier of Bernard's."

If Laura had been in the act of either eating or drinking, she would have had difficulty in not choking on a sharp spurt of laughter. A supplier, indeed. "Of leather," she suggested gravely, "or fabric?"

"Something like that." Poe's short thick fingers began to beat a tattoo on the arm of his chair, and as if reminded he made a focused study of Laura's left hand with its unaccompanied band of platinum. "You haven't lost your ring, I hope?"

He might be a wizard in the stock market, but he had just given himself away. "No, it's quite safe," said Laura, refusing to concoct any story about having the mounting checked. She found it all at once unendurable that he should sit there with his sly and privileged information about her marriage, Bernard content for him to have it, and view her wishfully as a murderess while holding her socially captive. "You'll have to excuse me now—"

There was a sudden commotion in the dining room: Max, in snowsuit and boots and mittens, saying imperatively, "We go park" and behind him Mrs. Wedge, apologetic: "I just couldn't contain him, Mrs. Fourte. For the last half hour he's been bound he'll have his outing."

A deliberate rescue mission, because the housekeeper hadn't liked being ticketed so bluntly for the hereafter? Whatever it was, Laura seized upon it. Poe waited with unmistakable significance while she put on her coat, but she had made up her mind that she was not going to resume the conversation broken off on the train.

She wasn't given an option. Outside on the doorstep, voice lowered as if the flanking old lilacs were wired for sound, Poe said, "About the matter we were discussing yesterday." His densely green-brown gaze flickered at her like a toad catching flies. "I'm onto something."

It was his exit line and his real reason for coming. He walked away without a pause to his Silver Shadow.

Irma had taught Max an elementary form of hide-and-go-seek, a fact for which Laura was not grateful. Much as she loved him, there were few things more tiresome than a repeated pretense of bewilderment, surprise, and admiration.

This afternoon, fortunately, a flight of crows came soaring and flapping into the highest branches of the hickories, ungainly but dramatic in their black studding. Max was persuaded to sit beside Laura and watch them, head tipped back, face rosy and absorbed, and in the silence barely broken by the muffled passing of an occasional car, round slaty juncos came hopping out of the evergreens and proceeded to the pond and the crumbs flung there.

Laura wondered for the first time if all that planting,

79

although it absorbed noise and no doubt exhaust fumes while providing a windbreak, was a very good idea in a park in which there were children, however infrequent. It would be no difficulty for someone to conceal himself among soft down-sweeping needles or clustering leaves, invisible from both within and without.

Instantly her mind presented her with a vision of Max, having adjured her in mysterious syllables that she wasn't to watch, burrowing excitedly into an iron grip, with a hand clamped swiftly over his mouth. Or herself, saying aloud, "Where can Max be?" and brushing aside branches not on a small child but a dangerous adult crouch and a face hidden by a ski mask. The slits for the eyes, the evil little padded hook for the nose.

And two entrances to—or exits from—the park; one at the south, the natural approach from the Fourte house, the other at the north. In between, the deaf stone benches, the blind drinking fountain, the birds who could not bear witness. Sturdy Mrs. Dalloway, upon whom Laura had been half counting since the train, obviously had an alternate exercise route. A stern medical directive would be insupportable if you had to pass the same trees, same houses, same suspicious dogs every day.

She shook herself literally out of her ugly fantasy, jumping up from the bench with a suddenness which scattered the juncos, putting down an imperative hand to Max. "Time to go home, it's freezing."

The crows cawed angrily overhead but only rearranged themselves, necks twisting and dipping; they were not yet ready for their night's safe sojourn in the town. Laura got herself and Max clear of the park with a sense of narrow escape which was a warning in itself.

She mustn't deprive him of his favorite place because of her own twitchy fear, her frightful new notion of poison seeping along the road and up the hill to shelter cunningly among the evergreens, not waiting specifically for her or Max but for anyone foolish enough to be there after a certain hour. They would simply have to come earlier, before there could be any suggestion of bruising to the light, any possibility of dusk or whatever it shrouded making a pounce.

It wasn't far to the house, but Laura picked Max up midway in order to cover the remaining distance faster. As she rounded the final curve the strip of orchard came into view and then, at the top of the gentle rise, an unfamiliar vehicle, a van, standing in front of the wide-open front door which spilled out brilliance although the late afternoon was only graying.

There was a violent stab just under her ribs—that other return, to a patrol car with its mute statement of something very wrong—until she remembered Delahanty saying that he knew of a van he could borrow. And there, the prayer not answered, came a station wagon, its turn signal flicking on.

Because of an oncoming car moving at a deliberate pace, Laura got up the drive ahead of the Fourtes. Delahanty, evidently having conferred with Mrs. Wedge, emerged between the lilacs, and a tall black boy got out of the van and opened its back. The crows, deciding to call it a day, flew over, low, with a beat of wings audible until the station wagon approached with a shift of gears. From somewhere close by there was a loud and echoing gunshot, and a unit of blackness came pitching and tumbling out of the sky.

Max screamed then, a rip of terror and horror and loss which stirred Laura's scalp and plunged into her bones with its terrible, unavoidable implication.

He knew.

He had been there.

Nine

Somehow, trembling with transferred shock, ignoring everything around her—Delahanty's tight and furious "Who in God's name—?"; the piercing glances of the Fourtes, as if the sight of him had sent Max into a hysteria which seemed to come from the soul as well as the lungs; the black boy's white-ringed stare; Mrs. Wedge's frightened face—Laura managed to mount the stairs with Max, repeating a lie which appalled her even as she uttered it.

"It's all right, Max, it's all right."

He was crying uncontrollably now, which he had not done on the afternoon when she had brought herself to say steadily, "Daddy is gone and he can't come back ever, but I'm here and I will take care of you. Will you help take care of me?"

In retrospect, he hadn't believed her. He had heard what would be a deafening noise inside a car, and seen blood, but until that helpless black plummet out of the air he had assured himself secretly that his father would survive the bewildering event.

So he had played with his mouse game and his nest of boxes, and chortled, and been angrily undone when Julian turned out to be himself and not Bernard.

Laura scarcely knew what to do with him, or how to

take in what this had to mean. She ran warm water into the bathtub, coped with the zipper of his snowsuit with fingers that shook, talked to him as inanely as if he were a difficult adult.

"Is this hot enough? Good." He was far too small to be left in a tub unattended, and Laura, on her knees beside it, swiveled around and found a box of tissues. "Let's blow your nose—there, isn't that better?"

Max was quieting. Laura did not dream of saying that the shot crow had been only a bird, because he loved birds, and neither could she think of questioning him. He was shattered for the moment, he had had all he could bear.

There was a tap at the bathroom door and Naomi looked in. It might have been the light that gave her eyes an odd deep shine. "Is there anything I can help with?"

It was unfair to be reminded of people who brought a certain greed to accident scenes. "No, thanks, we'll be down in a few minutes. I think food would be the best idea, so if you'd tell Mrs. Wedge . . ."

Was there any hope that, Naomi having had a chance to inspect her nephew for herself, she and Julian would be merciful and leave right away? No. Even in the midst of a reaction which she could still feel down to her toes, Laura had listened for and not heard the faint thud of the front door closing. Delahanty was still here, and they would outwait him.

She toweled Max dry, put him into the pajamas she had hung over the heated rail, got his bathrobe and slippers. Now he needs a pipe, she thought with a dangerous leaning toward lunacy.

No use pretending that nothing had happened. In fact, acknowledgment was essential. "Are you all right, Max? Shall we go and get your dinner?"

He consulted with himself, nodded, and gazed up at her out of Bernard's vividly gray eyes. "Daddy all gone," he said exploringly.

"Yes." The fact of death was finally clear to him, and Laura could only pray that he would not have nightmares about his father clad in black feathers. And that she would not. Had the spoon with its half aspirin and jam, the night he had stared transfixedly past her, looked flashingly like something else made of metal?

She would have to ask him, but not yet.

In the living room, Naomi was being intensely social with the black boy, insouciant in his tan leather motoring cap. The rocking horse in the study had been displayed; Julian, coming out, said over his shoulder, ". . . delightful. It will be an heirloom," and, after a rapid study of Laura and her charge, "Let me get you a drink."

Delahanty halted in the still-lighted doorway. "Lester, take off your hat." From his tone, half absent and half exasperated, he might have been addressing a much younger brother in constant need of chiding on the issue. He turned to Laura, his attention extraordinarily blue. "Could you come and see if you want this thing moved? Your housekeeper suggested the spot, but you'll have a little trouble getting at the window for a few days."

With Julian vanished, Naomi had no choice. She said to Lester, "Do excuse me," and rose. "Come along, Max, and we'll see what Mrs. Wedge has for you."

Laura was into the study in a twinkling, scarcely noticing that the door did not open as wide as usual because the rocking horse, retarpaulined, was behind it. She said tensely, "I'm so—Max saw it. He saw Bernard being killed."

"I thought it must be something like that." Delahanty's

folded arms were reminiscent of his pocketed hands in Toby Newell's office; he wasn't going to touch her and thereby ignite the atmosphere for two acute observers. "But unless I'm very much mistaken, Julian and his wife have a different explanation. With me in it."

"They were both in the room when Max came downstairs just now, and they must have seen that there was no reaction whatever."

"Because you swept him off in order to threaten or cajole or brainwash him, would be their answer to that. . . . Don't," said Delahanty, "be surprised at anything you hear about me in the next couple of days, will you?"

Voices in the dining room: Naomi and Julian were coming back. There wasn't time to inquire even with her eyebrows about that odd, deliberate choice of words, because now there was a lightly summoning "Laura?" She said clearly to Delahanty, as if in answer to the matter of the semiblocked window, "No, that won't be any problem," and they went out into the living room.

Her drink was waiting, and the Fourtes had theirs. Delahanty and Lester were asked by Julian as functioning bartender if they wouldn't have something. Delahanty declined for them both with matching courtesy, said goodnight, and had the front door closed behind them before any ushering-out could be done.

Into the tiny preliminary silence which is apt to follow any departure, Naomi said meditatively, "He's really quite attractive, isn't he?"

It wasn't like her to be clumsy. Laura said, "He is, rather," in a tone which conveyed a genuine brushing-aside. The further implications of Max's witnessing, obscured until now by shock, had leaped at her.

Such as: How many people knew that he was more inarticulate than most two-year-olds? Because he had certainly not been on that scene by accident.

Queerly, she had been concentrating on who had *not* killed Bernard, or setting out for herself the broad reasons why someone of either sex had reached the point where a mixture of rage and jealousy could not be contained. She had never thought in terms of a single known face, one to which she might have said, "Thank you for coming," in the days immediately after the murder.

She started to speak, but Julian was ahead of her. "I suppose the McWethy boys were at the bottom of that unfortunate incident."

The McWethys were Laura's nearest neighbors. Their young sons were handsome, amiable, and born lawbreakers; the stiff fine and possible jail sentence for discharging a firearm in this area would be simply a challenge to them. They had received automatic attention from the police even though the bullets which had killed Bernard had not been strays, but clearly one boy, who would be alibied by the other, had found the flight of crows irresistible.

"It was more than unfortunate," said Laura, and told them.

There were responses which seemed to go against nature—the overextended balloon bursting with a sigh, the flame sizzling along the fuse and dying harmlessly when it reached the charge—and this was one of them.

"But that's impossible," said Naomi calmly. She had shot Julian a peculiar glance while Laura was speaking. "The police had to pinpoint everybody in the house, naturally, to see if they had noticed anything unusual along the road before it happened, and Max was at the park with Irma. We gathered from Lieutenant Drexel that she had at least one witness to attest to that."

On the authority of Mrs. Wedge, Irma and Max had been home for approximately twenty minutes before the arrival of the first police car, and of course nobody, including Laura, had inquired about Max's mood. It had been one of the very few occasions when Laura had not seen him into his crib herself. Had Irma done that? Or Mrs. Wedge? Disaster tended to produce blank spots in familiar routine.

It was impossible to know exactly how long Bernard had been dead when a police cruiser made a routine check of the Mercedes parked on the shoulder. Its heater was efficient, and even with the ignition turned off the closed car would have retained some of its warmth. There were minutes involved here, although Laura's brain could not do any precise grappling.

"Max is so very bird minded," Naomi was saying now, making it sound like a tendency toward petty pilfering. "Perhaps you've passed that on to him unconsciously. After all, your father's Pulitzer book—"

The birds in *A Time for Owls* had been metaphorical, but Laura did not correct her and neither did Julian, although he controlled a slight and, to Laura, unprecedented grimace. He said, "You don't think that *Irma* killed Bernard?"

His incredulity encompassed a great deal, because there could have been only one motive for the girl. Even if she were ravishing, and she was far from that, Bernard would never have trifled with a servant in his own house. It would have been in execrable taste; even worse than the kind of socks which, with the legs crossed, revealed an unappetizing expanse of bare male leg.

"No, I don't," said Laura, "but somehow Max saw it. There is no other explanation for his reaction."

The cigarette box on the coffee table caught her eye interestingly. It was the kind which kept tobacco fresh for quite a while.

"Laura," said Naomi with the daintiness of water dropping on stone, "you don't realize it—you can't, you're too close to the situation—but this house is absolutely full of tension, and it's no wonder that Max was so frightened when he cut himself. His tantrum this afternoon was another example. That's why we thought from the beginning—all right," at the militant lift of Laura's head, "let that go, but there's something else you're overlooking."

There was a lighter beside the cigarette box, and that handy ashtray on the step. All at once Laura's drink, which had had time to turn watery, wanted punctuating.

"You're not home all the time, even on weekends," said Naomi. In this generally unhatted age, very few women could carry off a dramatic swerve of black felt over a dove-gray wool dress and a strand of pearls, but she managed it. "Max may very well have had opportunities of—hearing or even seeing Bernard threatened, days before. That stupid gunshot put the lid on it."

Back to you, Delahanty. Laura did not surprise herself by lighting her first cigarette in almost two years. It ought to have tasted dizzying and disgusting; it was heartening instead. Her utter conviction wasn't being accepted because they had their own version and they did not want it disturbed in any way.

Very well; proceed with caution. "I suppose it's possible, but I would have thought that Mrs. Wedge, who is permanently in residence and was very devoted to Bernard—"

"And, if I recall rightly, takes an after-lunch nap every day," said Julian, bending his brilliant gray glance on her.

There was something chilling about their determination, and they were quietly satisfied by Laura's cigarette, the tangible evidence of nerves. To put it out prematurely, even though two inhalations had been enough, would be an underscoring.

Because of the tautness in the room, Mrs. Wedge's voice was startling. "Shall I get Max ready for bed, Mrs. Fourte?"

He stood beside the housekeeper, hand reached trustfully up to hers, sleep-struck by new knowledge, warm bath, food. "Would you, Mrs. Wedge? I'll be up in a few minutes. Oh, by the way"—it had to be done and right now, in spite of an uncomfortable thud of pulses—"I forgot to ask Mr. Delahanty if he'd been up to talk to my husband during the past several days. Was he, do you know?"

"Not that I'm aware of." Mrs. Wedge's voice was wooden; she must not have cared for the bruiting-about of her well-deserved naps. "Aren't you going to say goodnight to your aunt and uncle, Max?"

Max yawned, and it made him shiver. "Good-night," he said.

Naomi and Julian got into their coats, declining another drink and Laura's automatic invitation to stay for dinner; it was getting late and they were expecting people that evening. They had put Christmas presents in the top of the coat closet although they would see Laura before the day itself.

With the arrival of darkness, there was no question of Julian's driving the Mercedes away with Naomi following. At the door, he said to Laura, "You'll have to do as you think best, of course, but I don't know that I'd mention your theory about Max to the police."

Laura had never intended to. It was real, grisly newspaper material: "Did Tot View Slaying?"

She reassured Julian, said good-night, closed the door, leaned briefly against it with a temptation to put her face in her hands. But, even to spare Max, a casual, quiet questioning could not be put off any longer; that would be tantamount to giving Bernard's killer a parting salute. Dreading every step of the way, she went upstairs.

Ten

Mrs. Wedge had been keeping an ear cocked, and intercepted Laura in the hall. It was clear from her faintly scandalized manner that she had not realized Max's reaction to the gunshot to be any more complex than fright at an unexpected noise and the loss, before his eyes, of something alive.

"Think of it," she said, obviously having been interrupted in soothing talk about Christmas. "He doesn't want Santa Claus to come down the chimney."

Hardly; there had been enough damage done to his life without oddly named strangers penetrating the house in such an outlandish fashion—and while he slept, at that. There wasn't time to go into it. "All right," said Laura. "I'll say that everything gets left outside the front door and you and I wake up very early and bring it in."

Mrs. Wedge pursed her lips in disapproval of the abandonment of tradition and changed the subject. "I thought a nice lamb chop and creamed potatoes with lemon broccoli."

All her proposals for dinner were couched in the past tense. Laura agreed without really hearing, said that she wanted at least half an hour, and proceeded to Max's room.

He was in the armchair with his alphabet book. As

always when he emerged from the housekeeper's hands, his small features appeared to have been buffed, his hair painted on. Laura did not join him in the chair at once, because then she would not have been able to see his face, but went to the curtained window instead and fiddled briskly with one of the levers.

That what she had to do was necessary for more than one reason was of no particular help. It might be necessary to remove a tumor, too, but what if you had never held a scalpel before? The sum total of her experience of children sat regarding her expectantly with drowsy gray eyes, and as with most things there must be a right way and a wrong way to go about this.

"That was a very loud bang this afternoon when we got home," said Laura, and added, although there were varieties which had hideous manners around wounded animals, "It's wrong to shoot birds."

Max nodded solemnly at her. "Bird all gone."

Where had the crow fallen? On the McWethy property, it was to be hoped. "Was it a very loud bang in Daddy's car?"

Max shrank a little. The bob of his head was fractional and curiously adult, as if at a trespasser.

Certain though Laura had been, it was instinctive to close her eyes tightly as she thought of the cruelty imposed on a small child, premeditatedly, in the one sure way to ambush Bernard on the road. "Who was with you, Max?"

He didn't seem to comprehend that; his expression said that as his whole existence was ordered by other people, Laura ought to know better than he.

"You went to the park with Irma"—more wielding of the inexperienced scalpel—"and then someone took you for a walk along the road to meet Daddy. It wasn't Irma, because she stayed in the park. Was it a friend?"

Max comprehended a great many more words than he could say, but he was embattled. How long was five days to a two-year-old mind when sudden shock was thrown into an accustomed pattern of life? Laura, fully cognizant of clocks and calendars, had nevertheless known periods of time which spent themselves like lighted cellophane and others which had an air of infinity.

"Was it a lady, Max, or was it a man?"

But she had driven him too far back toward a scene which he did not want to remember, and his earlier touch of reserve became hostility. Was it an infant form of guilt because he had been present but unable to prevent a death as swift and sure as the crow's? He was rough with his treasured book; he turned the pages with a creasing and mashing effect and said angrily, "Lobster."

Pursuing the matter just now would be worse than pointless, but he could not be left like this. Laura sat down in the armchair and took him placatingly on her lap, wishing that she had an alphabet book of her own to show him. *P* is for *Persian lamb* . . .

No, go back. *N* is for *Naomi*.

It vaulted lightly and easily into her mind. She didn't examine it closely but neither did she recoil from it, if only because anyone whom Naomi wanted dead would arrive at that state with a minimum of fuss. And she was by no means an intimate of Max's world; he had usually been in bed on the Fourtes' infrequent visits, and any detailed knowledge of him had been passed idly along from Bernard to Julian.

Had it been Naomi from whom he had flinched that afternoon?

Gradually Max's small body lost its rigidity inside the bankerish stripes of blue and gray and white flannel. Laura put him into his crib, bestowed a kiss, wheeled one side of the casement window open, and switched off the light.

When you were balked on one front the only thing to do was approach from another direction. Laura went downstairs and through the silent living room into the study. The telephone number Mrs. Wedge had given her was still on the desk, under "Irma" in her own handwriting, and she dialed it.

The ringing at the other end went on for so long that she was about to put the receiver back when a feminine voice said reluctantly, "Hello?"

"Is Irma there?" Under the new circumstances, identification seemed unwise.

"Nope." Jauntiness and a certain satisfaction were combined in a single syllable.

"Could you tell me when she might be in?"

"Never, I don't guess." An atmosphere of doom was erased at once by what sounded like a miniature scuffle, an arch giggle and an adjuration to stop that. "She moved out."

No, she didn't know when or where. She had waked to an empty house and a note from Wendy, the other girl who lived there, to the effect that they would have to find a new co-tenant before January first. That was all she knew and, at an impatient male voice in the background, she had to hang up now.

"Will Wendy be in this evening?" It was like a pay

phone in London: if you did not speak at the precise time, you lost your chance.

"Prob'ly, but she's working till nine. Bye," said the girl, effectively wiping out Laura's beginning "Where—" and vanished upon a click and a dial tone.

Could Irma's departure be not so much sudden as the fulfilling of plans confided to her aunt weeks or even months ago and only waiting for circumstances to fall into place?

But Mrs. Wedge, mutely commanding cream sauce to behave itself in the double boiler while she put broccoli into the steamer and a lamb chop under the grill, shook her head critically. "Three girls living together makes a vicious triangle."

She tipped diced cold baked potatoes into the cream sauce, turned the flame to pinpoint level, and produced a lemon wedge for readiness as if the broccoli had suddenly spoken to her. "I didn't know whether you wanted me to say so, Mrs. Fourte, but Mr. Delahanty *was* here on—it would have been the day before."

How many implications in that simple statement? Laura was so dazzled by the revelation that the housekeeper's loyalty to the Fourtes was not the blind and blanket affair it had seemed that she could only wait.

Mrs. Wedge inspected the lamb chop and adopted a narrative style. "You were off to have your hair cut that afternoon, and they kept you waiting. It must have been after five when Mr. Delahanty drove up and Mr. Fourte let him in. I was drawing the curtains in the dining room"—

Bernard hadn't mentioned it, thought Laura in seconds

of deafness, although she might well have encountered Delahanty's unknown car in the course of her return home.

—"and Mr. Fourte said something like, 'If it's my wife
you wanted, I'm afraid you're too early,' and Mr. Delahanty said that people who didn't answer their telephones
could expect visitors sooner or later. They sounded friendly
and unfriendly, if you know what I mean." Courteous
voices; yes. "Irma had Max in the living room, so they went
into the study."

For all the straightforwardness of this exposition, it
seemed to Laura that something curious had slipped into
the kitchen. Was it merely the fact that the housekeeper,
often invisible in her competence, had always had her own
views and sympathies? However undetectably, there
would be people she liked and people she didn't.

"I think there was stuffed Cornish game hen and snow
peas that night," said Mrs. Wedge, giving the creamed
potatoes a judicious stir, "and I was busy with those for it
might have been ten minutes. When I went in to draw the
living room curtains they must have been just ready to
come out of the study, because I couldn't help hearing
them. Mr. Fourte mentioned a bed of roses and Mr. Delahanty said a contract was a contract and he'd fulfilled his
part of it."

The door of the grill was opened and the lamb chop
turned. "Not long now," said Mrs. Wedge with an unmistakable finality. She had completed her recital without losing an iota of her grandmotherly look and would prefer to
be left alone, like a midwife, for the final browning and the
lemon-buttering of the broccoli.

Laura returned to the living room feeling as if she had

seen a familiar landscape in a dramatically altering light. Mrs. Wedge had obviously kept Delahanty's visit from the police. Why? Because even on slight acquaintance she believed him to be incapable of murder?

Don't listen to the voice reminding that in a deviation from custom, Mrs. Wedge had monitored the telephone for those first few unstrung hours, and the contention of cynics that everybody had a price.

Almost everybody, perhaps. Not Mrs. Wedge. Being the woman she was, she must have felt wordlessly demeaned by Bernard's unaccompanied evenings out and late returns home, and from the angry color in her cheeks she had had a sense of insult at the actual presence of Persian lamb, studied arrogance, alien perfume.

Mrs. Cleef, or Creef. Neither, thought Laura, wandering up to Alan Petrie's hyacinths. Homer Poe, protecting Bernard, had offered the first syllable which came into his head when he was taken by surprise and then added another by way of more dust throwing. Whatever her actual identity, Bernard would certainly have stopped the Mercedes for her or any other unlikely person holding his child by the hand.

But not for Irma, except in the case of a downpour which hadn't existed. He had approved of regular exercise for Max and liked the idea of the park, where it could be hoped that other small children might be encountered, even though he had dismissed Laura's concern about the lack of peer companionship: "You grew up among adults, and it didn't do you any harm."

Laura, remembering her self-punishing months because she had survived those unspeakable seconds in London and her father had not, was far from sure.

Would Irma, properly approached, have turned Max over to someone else for a few minutes?

Yes, if the someone had been entertained at the Fourte house. Or even—the maid was readily impressed by furs or jewelry or any other symbol of importance—if the recognition was one-sided but appeared sure.

"Little Max Fourte! He could scarcely toddle when I last saw him, and now look! There's a beautiful new crèche on a lawn not two minutes away, which he really should see. May I borrow him, and we'll be right back? Oh, I'm Mrs. . . ." Any name would do.

Would Max have gone willingly? Again, yes; he was a trusting and affectionate child, and would have taken Irma's permission as endorsement.

On the other hand, it could have been even simpler than that. Max playing his indefatigable hide-and-go-seek among the evergreens, Irma growing bored and falling into conversation with her witness, the minutes slipping by while Max was coaxed away—"Laura wants you"—and then returned.

With what kind of threat, although he must have been largely uncomprehending? A ferocity of eyes would explain to him, "I'll come and get you if you tell," or, better, "If you want Daddy to come back—"

A light shake of cold traveled over Laura; that kind of wickedness, to a child, came close to rivaling murder. And what had been said sympathetically to Irma later, after an apparent visit to Virgin and Child and Wise Men? "I don't think I'd mention . . . People get very excitable at these times and seize on trifles. Even Mrs. Fourte—"

Mrs. Wedge announced dinner, tonight accompanied by a glass of red wine. There was something indefinably odd about seeing in its finished state a meal viewed with distraction in its separate parts. The chop was crisply brown, the broccoli a bouquet of vivid lemony green; the potatoes had paid a visit to the grill and carried miniature peaks of gold.

Laura, complimenting the housekeeper as usual, took a further step with a new wariness as she unfolded her napkin. "I'm glad Max is over his cold or whatever it was. I suppose he was coming down with it on Friday night and I didn't notice."

"He might have been a little flushed, but he usually is after his walk. I only saw him for a minute before Irma took him upstairs, and he said, 'Where Daddy?' and it wasn't very long before Mr. Fourte could be expected so I said, God help me," said Mrs. Wedge, her eyes filling again at the table set for one, "that he'd see his father after his bath."

And there it was, the last little piece of that particular puzzle. Mrs. Wedge had been a pillar of Max's world since his earliest awareness, and authority could not be wrong. In spite of what he had seen in the Mercedes, it was only a matter of waiting for his father to come back.

Laura had brought her book to the table, a years-long habit when she dined alone, but she did not make a great deal of headway with it. She had given Delahanty an oblique promise that she would not believe any suggestive things about him which might surface in the immediate future, but she had expected those to come by way of the Fourtes rather than Mrs. Wedge.

"A bed of roses." Something prickled there, just around the corner from recognition. And "A contract is a contract," with Delahanty having carried out his part of it.

Not the kiss in the taxi. Not something begun as a test and then getting out of hand.

Laura's mind, shying away from both references, fastened upon something else so obvious that it had slid right past her. Irma's witness, the "at least one" mentioned so crisply by Naomi; the apparent certification that she, and by extension Max, had been in the park all through the crucial interval.

Well, there was a perfectly good explanation for that. Go to the park tomorrow, weather permitting, and test it for herself. Meanwhile, as soon after nine o'clock as was practical, call Wendy before she could join Irma in some crevice with the truth pulled in after them.

Laura did better than that. At a little after nine-thirty, and at her own suggestion, Wendy came to the house.

Eleven

She was a pale, angular girl with a mass of carefully frizzed blond hair framing a narrow, discontented face, and from the moment of arrival it was clear that a driving curiosity rather than any real knowledge had brought her here. Her full name proved to be Wendy Hilliard.

Thanked for coming, she said with a disparaging glance at Laura's tailored shirt and pink tweed skirt, "Well, I was dressed," and dressed she was, in long earrings, embroidered vest over balloon sleeves, flounces reaching to mid-shin. She had taken one open and devouring look around her as she crossed the threshold; the rest of her inspection was conducted in darting, secretive glances.

"Can I get you something to drink?" asked Laura when the girl had settled herself on the couch. Unsure of the schedule of someone who worked until nine, she had put out a plate of crackers and cheese and a dish of olives.

Wendy lifted her lashes from a racing examination of the rug and the legs of all the furniture, announced that she would have a martini, and, by the time Laura came back with it and a tall glass of beer for herself, largely as prop, had assumed a subtly different air; one of petty command. After all, she was in possession of the information wanted.

She took a sip of her martini. "So, you want to hear about Irma."

"To get in touch with her, yes."

A good friend of Irma's might have inquired guardedly why, and Laura could trot out the sent check and a scruple about not having taken the cold seriously enough, but neither was necessary; Wendy didn't qualify. "She's gone to New York," she said, "to see—are you ready for this?—a talent scout who's interested in her."

The irresistible lure: according to Mrs. Wedge, Irma had had dreams of a movie career ever since appearing as a dot in a filmed crowd scene. Personal knowledge of that wasn't necessary, given the rehearsed and regal display of the neck. The ploy had probably begun shortly after the dawn of recorded history, with the grunted equivalent of "I beg your pardon, but have you ever considered? . . ."

"I mean, *Irma*? Can you imagine?" Wendy, who had sat back triumphantly on the couch, was dissatisfied with Laura's reaction, or lack of it. "She told me she'd had a small part in a movie once and I said, 'Playing what, a snake?'" She was pleased with her repartee. "There's this boyfriend, Frank something. Maybe she had to leave town for a while."

Laura, who had been uncharitable about Irma's preening neck, nevertheless said to herself, speaking of snakes— "I should have tried to reach her sooner. When did the talent scout call, do you know?"

"I think it was Friday night, because she sprang it after I had to ask her not to use my blow-dryer," said Wendy, fingering her frizzy hair with pride. All at once, she sharpened. "Wasn't that the day your husband got killed?"

Her hungry glance was natural enough; still, Laura confined herself to a nod.

"The thing is, Irma talked all the time but she had these moods where if you didn't sit on the edge of your chair she'd close up like a clam. She wouldn't say another word to me last night, she just packed her stuff and took off before I got up. Leaving Mildred and I high and dry," added Wendy censoriously.

New York, the ideal disappearing place. Equally, a magic name to the young and ambitious. Irma had been sent, Laura was sure of it, to isolate her from any further questioning by the police or anyone else—and carefully not at once, because the immediate vanishing of a girl connected with the Fourte household would have given rise to suspicion. Money must have changed hands, decorously—"Call it a loan"—as on her salary she could not have saved enough to support her for any length of time in the city—unless, of course, she had relatives there.

But Wendy, queried, shook her head positively; she was sure Irma would have waved that in their faces. At the same time she gave her empty glass a nudge in Laura's direction, indicating that she had something further to say. Provided with a fresh drink, she rewarded Laura by extending a small silver pillbox, its lid set with an aquamarine. "Is this yours?"

There was no need for a closer examination. "No."

"Good, I'll keep it," said Wendy with great simplicity. "It fell out of Irma's coat pocket when she was dumping things around on her bed last night."

The implication being that Irma had stolen it, which she would never have done. She wasn't brilliant or even very energetic, but neither was she a thief. She had either

104

found it somewhere or it was part of what she didn't recognize to be a bribe.

"You know something?" Wendy narrowed her eyes confidentially. "She didn't go to the doctor the way she said she did. I thought there was something fishy about it, she wasn't that sick, and it was my day off, so when she was upstairs taking a shower I called his office and said my friend had left a scarf in the waiting room. She hadn't been there at all."

What a horror this girl must be to live with—but if there had been the slightest doubt as to whether Irma's departure from Burnbrook had been masterminded, this took care of it. She had been enjoined to secrecy about a mission connected with the coming trip—plausibly; people doing apparent favors did not care to think of a steady stream of applicants.

But, necessary though the interview had been, a delicate ugliness had begun to invade the air; Laura felt suddenly as sly as Wendy. She said, reaching for her second cigarette in two years as if any small brisk action might help to speed the visitor on her way, "When Irma gets in touch with one of you, could you let me know?"

"Oh, she won't be doing that," said Wendy, but again the black echo was quickly quieted. "You know what'll happen? She'll fall on her face in New York and have to take up waitressing or something, and she certainly won't report that. Or if she does write, it'll be a whole bunch of lies about hobnobbing with actors and actresses and there won't be a return address, so that nobody can go and check up on her."

She couldn't help it, Laura realized; she was so sharp and curdled that she wished no good for anyone. Too bad there was such an age differential; she would have made a suitable companion for Homer Poe. Even suspecting what she did about Irma's unwitting instrumentality in Bernard's death, Laura, standing, felt compelled to say, "Who knows? Irma may surprise us all."

As she spoke, Homer Poe was in the process of being killed.

He was pleased, on the whole, when the wild theory he had been flirting with ever since his visit to Laura Fourte that afternoon was cut to the ground by means of a simple telephone call. "Collect, I insist," said his visitor, and although he was already half convinced of his error, Poe was a man to whom no one had to say "Collect" twice.

There had been a bad few seconds when he opened his front door to the unheralded knocking, something he rarely had to do. The defection of two wives had inspired in him a fierce hatred of anything resembling domesticity, and with the inclusion of the handsome house on Pelham Hill in the second divorce settlement he had rented this small, comfortless, and somewhat shabby place.

Although a cleaning woman came once a week, Poe used the house solely as a base of operations. Here he slept, telephoned his broker, occasionally heated a frozen dinner. The rest of the time he dined out, visited friends, and repaid their hospitality—when he could; often they seemed to be very busy—in restaurants.

Now, putting down the receiver, somewhat a disadvantage in these undistinguished surroundings, he said stiffly, "It would appear that I owe you an apology."

"Perhaps it's understandable. I have no way of knowing."

But Poe had been as graceful as he intended to be, and had no use for further discussion or, for that matter, company. He was anxious to get back to his original conviction, absence having made the heart grow fonder, and to align the sequence of events for official presentation. Without being aware of it, he adopted the expression of a frog deep in suspicious thought.

Laura and the designer, Delahanty, lunching at the restaurant where Poe, seated at an unobtrusive table, had been able to watch them in a mirror. Something going on there; they had the air of two people on a desert island.

A few days later, with the full light from his office window striking his cheekbone, Bernard volunteering the astonishing information that Delahanty had erupted at him the evening before outside a Greenwich Village hotel.

Poe, aghast: "You brought charges, of course."

Bernard: "With the police what they are these days? I'd have paid him back on the spot, but he turned out to have a gun. I'd rather you kept that to yourself for the moment."

And, spinning to profile in his chair: "Something's breathing cold on my neck, Homer."

After that, Delahanty an inexplicable presence at the Fourte, Inc., cocktail party, although he would have had to contain himself in the midst of forty people. Not in the best of tempers, however; coolly ignoring the properly accompanied caviar nestled in ice, the tiny triangular Smithfield ham sandwiches, the little golden squares of pastry containing sherried chicken with Parmesan cheese. Apart from civility to customers approaching him, he had spoken only to Laura.

On the following Friday, Bernard decoyed to a fatal stop on his way home from the station.

Poe knew dispassionately that if she really set about it, Laura would have had no difficulty in obtaining a divorce, but why should she—and Delahanty—settle for less than Bernard's entire estate?

His brows drew with his determination to remain on the sidelines no longer. His visitor said, "Is that your cat at the window?"

Poe neither owned a cat nor encouraged any in the neighborhood, but the swing of his head to the right was automatic. Something punched him in the chest like the heel of a driving hand; his ears filled with sound; there wasn't time to complete his incredulous clutching at himself. When the sound was repeated he was in a different position, the lighted ceiling reeling over him into a dissolve. He did not feel the swift inquiring finger at neck and then at wrist; he was seconds beyond ever feeling anything again.

Queried the next morning, the Cheadles, across the road and twenty yards up, said that although their procession of television programs contained some gunshots, they had nevertheless gone to glance slantingly at the curtained front windows of Poe's house at nine-thirty or ten; they couldn't agree as to time. The driveway was empty and, while they watched, the downstairs lights went serenely out, one by one.

No, it hadn't occurred to them to call. Poe wasn't particularly friendly and they had assumed that he was on his way to bed.

Mrs. Cheadle, who fired off to various publications poetry which returned as faithfully as a boomerang from an expert hand, said inspiredly, "To his final rest he went, by a cruel bullet sent."

108

Her husband said glumly, "I wish you wouldn't do that, Alice."

Max had been crying, and at some length; the soft light from the hall picked up the dull shine of wandering tear tracks and ineffectual smears. Laura knew that millions of children all over the world had seen and endured far worse, but he was Max and this was here and now and she felt wrenched. He was, without being in the least dull about it, such an extremely good little boy.

Tomorrow she would have to subject him to questioning again, and for purposes of elimination show him the never-worn astrakhan hat presented to Bernard by his brother-in-law—and then, no matter what Mrs. Wedge's outrage, she would give him his rocking horse if the circumstances warranted it. The saving of the pièce de résistance for Christmas morning was, in the case of a two-year-old, a matter of pleasure for adults rather than the child's. And he needed something, a large exotic something, to pass into his world like a jolt of electric current.

Laura left his tear marks alone for fear of waking him fully to their cause, carried him out of the bathroom, returned him to his crib. This time she closed his door instead of leaving it a few inches open. Wendy had had such a sapping effect that she would come up to bed herself after she had carried out a mission which wasn't really peculiar in its urgency.

Although the housekeeper never asked questions, her expression would. At the customary eight-thirty, bound for her television set and ultimate slumber, she had left Laura alone in the living room. In all probability she had never met Wendy and could not know her proclivity for spying;

still, Irma had become chancy ground for all Mrs. Wedge's detached observations about her niece and it seemed simpler to erase all trace than to invent another guest.

Laura took the glasses and cheese plate and olive dish to the kitchen and washed and dried and put them away, ridiculously careful of clicks and jostles. She disposed of the beer can, replaced the gin and vermouth in the liquor cabinet in the dining room; even, like someone cleaning up after a crime, emptied and wiped clear the ashtray she had used so briefly.

She should not have allowed such a reference to cross her mind, because at once she was seized by the illogical fear that had visited her at the mailbox in the snowy dark; the sensation of a murderous stare homing in. She had locked the front door after Wendy's departure, but had Mrs. Wedge—?

Yes. The back door was also locked, the folds of ticking that masked its pane comfortable and unstirring. Laura darkened the kitchen and headed for the living room to do the same there; just as she had been on her exposed way up the hill, she was afraid to actually run. In a matter of minutes she would be safely upstairs in bed, reading, with other trusted presences only a few yards away. Even sleepers were company of a kind.

In the intense silence which she had helped weave, the telephone springing to life had the quality of a beast bursting from underbrush. Laura, unstrung at the end of a long and shocking day, nearly cried out, but clipped her palms hard against her cheeks instead and began to count the rings.

Twelve

And the possibilities, as the ringing continued.

. . . Two. Delahanty? She was too spent for that; she would say the wrong thing and it might prove irrevocable.

. . . Three. Naomi or Julian? They knew she wasn't an early retirer and would assume triumphantly, if the telephone went unanswered, that Delahanty's leaving had been a feint and Laura was with him somewhere.

. . . Four. The Persian-lamb woman, with another drop of venom?

. . . Homer Poe? "I'm onto something."

. . . Six. Wendy? She had had more than enough time to reach home and might have been spurred to make a further search of Irma's room or discarded belongings.

. . . Seven. Wild thought: her mother, whom she hadn't seen in fifteen years and to whom word of Bernard's death might have percolated on one of the Greek islands?

Laura could stand it no longer; she cut into the eighth ring in a tone which reflected her embattlement.

"Mrs. Fourte." Somehow Lieutenant Drexel had never entered her head. His voice came close to crackling with cold. "I asked you at the outset if your husband had quarreled with anyone recently and you said no. I also asked you if there was a friend in whom he might have confided such a matter, and you denied that too."

His choice of words had a witness-stand echo, and a bone-pressing headache sprang upon Laura's forehead with the ease and suddenness of a fly alighting there. "I didn't—"

She was not to be allowed to speak yet; the bombardment wasn't over.

"I now discover, at this very late date, that there had been a scuffle between your husband and one of his employees, and that in fact your husband had felt his life to be threatened for days before his actual death. We have—finally—taken a statement from Mr. Thomas Delahanty, and I have warned all parties concerned, with the exception of Mr. Homer Poe, whom I will take care of tomorrow, that the withholding of relevant information in a murder investigation is a serious matter."

It had flickered through Laura's mind that it was peculiarly difficult to think of Delahanty as anybody's employee; with a suggestion of courtesy rather than arrogance, he seemed to be where he was because it pleased him.

Her headache deepened. She said with an iciness as crisp as Drexel's, "May I? As to feeling his life threatened, my husband never mentioned a word to me or to his brother, whom he saw regularly at Fourte in New York. As to an altercation with Mr. Delahanty, it can't have been all that serious or he wouldn't have been at the company cocktail party at my husband's behest."

Drexel did not comment that astounding cracks were routinely papered over in the interests of commerce. "You think, then, that Mr. Poe simply made up the business about your husband feeling threatened?" Thoughtful, credulous, inviting more lies.

The oak staircase was sturdy, but there were undoubtedly slippered feet starting down it. Laura closed her eyes and uttered a silent curse. She said, "I think Mr. Poe is somewhat obsessed by the Fourte family."

"But he could be regarded as a close friend of your husband's?"

Laura suspected that that wasn't a precise definition: Homer was so handed down, so accustomed to, that apart from his sprinkle of market tips he had the it-doesn't-matter air of a barber or, in the case of women, a hairdresser. She was enormously tired, and she wished stalwart Mrs. Wedge in perdition. "Yes."

There was a pause at the other end of the line, and then: "If you have anything else to tell me, Mrs. Fourte, I advise you to do so now."

Throw him something, thought Laura. Max, who had made the difficult journey back from hostility to trust and fallen vulnerably asleep in her presence even though he had cried later? Experts would know how to gouge at him. Never mind the repeated pain and some bleeding; the tender flesh would heal.

Laura didn't have to see it, because they wouldn't let her. They would, sensibly, take away his sure support before they started.

The time might come when she had to drive a bargain with Drexel, but it hadn't yet. She said, "There is one thing . . ." and gave him—safely; Mrs. Wedge had been in the kitchen at the time—an edited version of the visit from the woman for whom Homer Poe had established such a ludicrous identity. She ended, "A woman who declined to give her name might very well make an anonymous telephone call to the police."

"It's possible," said Drexel noncommittally, "but she would scarcely have turned up at your house if it involved much of a risk."

A notion so eccentric as to be logical under the circumstances shot into Laura's mind. On the verge of an impulsive "Hold on a minute," she remembered that from a neutral menace this man had turned into a slightly more positive one. She said good-night, hung up, and went rapidly into the study.

There was nothing interesting under the A's in the address book she had shared with Bernard, but he had kept a smaller and separate one which had to do with all aspects of Fourte, Inc., including a list of long-time customers to whom imported wines or baskets of fruit were dispatched at Christmas. And here, unspecified as to gender, was H. Arpels, with an address near Gramercy Park.

"Mrs. Cleef, or Creef." Homer Poe, taken off balance and determined to protect Bernard, and perhaps subconsciously influenced by the new absence of Laura's engagement ring, had put together most of the names of old and well-known jewelers.

At the sound of Mrs. Wedge in her circumspect approach, Laura slid both address books back into their drawer as if she had been prowling through a diary and was on her feet and moving toward the door when the housekeeper appeared.

"I'm sorry to bother you, Mrs. Fourte, but Max is awake and he feels quite warm. I thought you might want to have a look at him."

Was the low fever circling back of its own accord or had Laura roused it from its dormancy? Her headache now seemed to have burrowed inside the bone. "I'll be right there."

But, out of an impulse she couldn't define, she took twenty seconds first to return to the desk, open the drawer, and consult the *D*'s in the company address book. Delahanty's name was there with his address and telephone number, in ink like the other entries. Directly beneath, another and obviously penciled address and telephone number had been erased.

Thermostat lowered, lamps switched off. In the upstairs hall, the housekeeper's door was closed, Max's stood wide. Laura took a quiet step into the dim wash of light and stopped with sharpness. She had to fight an instinct to flee.

Mrs. Wedge had said that Max was awake, but that was far too passive a description. He lay on his back, his head turned toward the door, one hand gripping a crib bar. His eyes were wide open and he was smiling at almost jack-o'-lantern length, so that the silky, tearless curve of his cheek was accented. For two or three jarred heartbeats he looked serenely and utterly corrupted, as if he had not only learned to live with his knowledge but to enjoy and feed upon it.

Then he said an approximation of "Santa Claus," and everything fell sanely into place. The application of a washcloth was second nature to Mrs. Wedge, and she had admonished him to be a good boy while she went to get his mother, because Santa Claus was coming.

"Not yet, Max, but soon." Tingling with shame and a new fear of herself, Laura turned on the light and peeled the covers back to inspect his chest for any sign of rash. Her assessment of his heat and flush was automatic; what occupied her attention bitterly was the fact that Bernard's murderer had managed a fringe benefit of unguessed proportions.

Max understood a great deal more than he was able to put into words, and his throat didn't hurt, or his ears, or any other part of him. He didn't have to tell Laura that his appetite and his energy were normal. She gave him a half aspirin, using the opportunity to take two of her own, and, avoiding any mention of the chimney, talked quietly to him about Christmas.

She and Mrs. Wedge had agreed that there should be a tree, not the ceiling-high spruce Bernard had planned for this year, but a smaller one for the space between the two end living room windows now occupied by a table. Brought in and decorated on Christmas Eve after Max was asleep, it would still, to two-year-old eyes, be a magical creation. He was content presently to have his light extinguished and his door, unusually, left a little open for the night.

Laura felt flogged by the day, and when she was in bed after the sketchiest of preliminaries she put her pillow aside and lay perfectly flat for minutes, just breathing, not even thinking, as she supposed people must when they woke after prolonged surgery.

When she fell asleep, she didn't dream about Irma and the park, or Bernard crying hoarsely out of his black feathers, or even her momentary recoil from the child she loved, but about her mother.

A late morning in summer at the house in Westport loaned by a friend of Robert Gillespie's in the hope that a few months in the country would start him writing again after a three-year dry spell. Laura, thirteen, preempted by her mother to pick, hull, and wash blackberries, because with the last of the eggs being used up for lunch, dinner would be toasted cheese sandwiches and fruit.

The garden had been their salvation ever since July. Out of it, because the tiny bank balance must not be touched except in case of genuine catastrophe, Kate Gillespie had produced a long chain of casseroles, ending upon an evening when, determined to let nothing go to waste, she had added diced chicken livers. They were currently off casseroles.

The kitchen window was open. A car door slammed, a taxi drove away, two men identifiable as Robert's agent and his editor began to pick their way up the narrow path almost hidden in knee-high grass. Their voices carried clearly through the mask of honeysuckle.

"Why don't they get a sheep?"

"Are you crazy? Kate would have four legs of mutton in no time."

It was doubtful whether Kate would ever have laughed at that, but now the abrupt cessation of the egg whisk in the yellow mixing bowl had such a pending quality that Laura was careful not to look up from the blackberries. There was a knock at the front door, and the egg whisk resumed. "They're your father's visitors," said her mother in the hard and careless voice which had made its first appearance a few months ago. "He can let them in."

And, after what seemed an eternity to Laura, Robert did. An hour crept by, after the first ten minutes of which Laura slid out the back door. Even though she had not seen the effect of the next-to-last straw being laid neatly on an invisible pile, the kitchen was a place she thought she was better away from.

The taxi returned, lifted voices on the sunny air indicated farewells, Laura went back inside with a handful of daisies she had picked. Her mother, hair as dark as hers brushed shiningly smooth and a trace of pink on her cheekbones, seized them from her and put them in a gray pottery jar for the center of the dining room table, over which she had whipped a nasturtium-colored cloth. The inwardness of all this went over Laura's head in her famished state, although by evening she had sorted it out.

Lunch was omelet with herbs and a narrow loaf of French bread baked the day before. Robert had to be called twice from the screened porch where his typewriter reposed on its rickety stand, and when he said "Delicious" after his first forkful he might as well have said "Wednesday." His dark blue gaze was at once blank and busy, as though behind it something was being spun.

"Well," said Kate presently in a voice which struck Laura as being like a yank on a leash. "What was that all about?"

" . . . The usual," said Robert after a trundling forty seconds.

That meant encouragement, Laura knew from discussions which had started two years ago when she was eleven. Reminders from the agent and editor about the very good reviews of the last book, the near-miss with the Literary Guild, the critics' opinion that Robert Gillespie was a writer to watch.

She didn't dare lift her eyes from her plate, or take another bite of even something as quiet as omelet, and so she missed the straw that broke everything: her father's windowpane contemplation of her mother, as if he had found himself at the table with a stranger who wanted to bother him with chat while he was trying to think.

"Rather long for that, wasn't it? Excuse me," said Kate, and rose in apparent search of something from the kitchen. Robert bent his head and plunged his hands into his hair, heavily graying although he was only forty-three, in a ravaged gesture. "I had it," he said in a strangled voice. "Oh, Christ, I had it, and now it's gone."

"Maybe it will come back," ventured Laura. Her mother's quick footsteps were on the stairs, but her father didn't seem to hear them. "You know how it is with a kaleidoscope?" he said, swinging around to face her and really seeing her. "You shift it very carefully, and you have a pattern with nice colors but too much going on, and you keep playing with it and finally, not often, you get exactly the shapes and colors that you wanted when you started out. And then somebody good and kind comes along and gives the whole thing a twist before you've even had a chance to look at it."

Laura had always understood him without conscious effort, but then she had no way of knowing what he had been like in the years when she was her own universe, heedless and absorbed. "Like a dream when you're only half asleep, and somebody wakes you up and you wish they hadn't."

"Pretty much." They both finished their omelet and mopped up matter-of-factly, but with an increasing unease. "I think," said Robert, "that you ought to go up and see if your mother needs you."

But Laura didn't have to. Kate was suddenly there in her one good summer suit, suitcase in hand. She looked direly beautiful. "Good-bye, Robert. I overheard you saying that you had had something. So have I."

Her fringed hazel gaze, so brilliant that at times it appeared backlit with gold, moved to Laura, finding its mirror image. "It's too soon to ask you to make a choice, Laura, even though I'm fairly sure what it would be."

She opened the door without drama, said ironically to her husband and child transfixed in their chairs, "Don't get up, but do tell Hal Nichols"—Nichols was Robert's agent— "that I *loathe* mutton."

The door closed behind her.

"Mutton?" said Robert dazedly to his daughter like a man hit over the head with a board. *"Mutton?"*

Laura came partly awake to a loud rustle of rain. There was no moral to the story. Her mother had ceded custody, vanished to California, and married an Italian film producer as soon as the divorce was final. From the occasional pictures which appeared of her aboard yachts among equally recognizable faces, casseroles and coping with spells of silence had gone forever out of her life.

It took Robert Gillespie years, scattered with successful books that left him discontented, to recapture the concept which had been sent into limbo over the omelet and the daisies and the nasturtium-colored tablecloth. When he did, it was his prize-winning *A Time for Owls*.

The rain stopped with sheared-off suddenness and a peculiar silence gripped the night. Laura, now dreamlessly asleep, was unaware of either. She got up late to the aftermath of an ice storm, a world of buried silver under a gray sky, and the news that Homer Poe had been found shot to death in his house.

Mrs. Wedge, who listened for the weather forecast every morning as attentively as if she were planning a camping trip, had heard it on the kitchen radio.

"Just like—" She broke off significantly as she poured Laura's coffee, although Max, kneeling on a chair at the table, was oblivious as he transferred marbles from a colander to a muffin tin whose cups had been mercifully muffled by scraps of old sheeting. "Poor man." There was a very faint, entirely human complacence as she added, "Little did he know, yesterday."

Seldom, thought Laura, had that commonplace held more irony. Homer Poe, wrapped in portentous secrecy as he stood outside with her on the step, had known or at least suspected enough to make his death a necessity.

Mrs. Wedge presented cinnamon toast with a commanding air—"Sugar is good for shock" she said in an eat-your-carrots voice—and Laura bit into it obediently. Shock, along with mechanical pity and a horror at such violence, was the right word. Even in death, which shed the kindest light of all, Homer Poe was not a man to evoke tears.

She said, "Do the police know when it happened?"

Mrs. Wedge shook her piled gray head, on which a few paling but indomitable streaks of rust remained. "All the report said was that he was found early this morning. Max was pouring his marbles into the colander, but there was something about several hours. Many's the time I've heard Mr. Poe say he liked to be in bed by ten o'clock, but if he was in bed, wouldn't they have said so?"

It hadn't been much after ten when Lieutenant Drexel had told Laura coldly about having taken a statement from Delahanty. His all-inclusive warning about withholding information had excepted Homer Poe; he had obviously tried that number and gotten no answer.

At least I was home all evening, thought Laura ignobly, and realized at once that there was only her word for that. Early-retiring Mrs. Wedge mightn't have heard the quiet departure of the Mustang if she had been watching television and Laura had done no door slamming, and as to Wendy Hilliard's visit at about nine-thirty, what better way to create the impression of not having left the house after dinner?

"Laura," said Max invitingly, having arranged the muffin tin to suit him, and she moved to inspect his surprisingly sure balance: big clear shooter in the center cup, five marbles each in the surrounding ones, not stuffily by color but a vivid mixture. Mrs. Wedge, joining her, said proudly, "No fleas there."

"Very pretty, Max." Then, shrinking from it because no shadow from yesterday remained on his clear pleased face, Laura hoisted him down from the chair. "Come on, you and I have things to do."

She wondered as she led the way to the study why the Fourtes hadn't called to find out if she had learned about Homer Poe's murder. Even if they weren't radio listeners, it was the kind of news which sent people to their telephones, and Naomi and Julian would be high on the list of other people to be informed. From the timing of events there had been a family consultation about implicating Delahanty officially; they had had to weigh the questions which would arise out of that.

Such as: What had impelled Delahanty to turn physically on Bernard and in effect throw his job to the winds?

Laura thought she knew, from Delahanty's firm silence

on the subject. Instead of coming upon Bernard compromisingly in the company of "a lady not his wife," he had found the company to be quite otherwise and reacted out of instinct on Laura's behalf. With Bernard forever unable to respond, the episode was closed.

Homer Poe, on the fringe of the family for so many years, would have known about the bisexuality just as he had known about H. Arpels, but reluctant admissions could not be dug out of a dead man.

The astrakhan hat waited on the chair behind the desk. Laura, picking it up unobtrusively and sitting down at the same time so that she would be able to watch Max, held it out to him. "Did you see a lady in a coat made of this, Max, the last time you saw Daddy?"

He was passingly frightened of it, so tightly black in the light from the big north window, but when he looked at it more closely he shook his head.

Something like it, then, thought Laura, although the half recognition wasn't necessarily of a coat. She said, "Wait a minute," and went out to the closet beside the living room fireplace. She put on her light beige raincoat. "Did you see a coat like this?"

"Yes," said Max.

His eyes were almost drowningly wide, and full of visions, but it was impossible to stop now.

"And a hat? . . ." Laura donned the astrakhan, willynilly. Naomi's swoop of black felt, sufficient to bring Bernard to a startled halt . . .

Terrible though it was, it had to be asked. "Was Aunt Naomi with you that day, Max, when Daddy was killed?"

Max began shaking his head alarmedly when the question was in mid-frame. He glanced wildly at his playpen,

123

the amiable prison which held his toys and meant that things were going on which did not concern him.

Laura took off hat and raincoat, dropping them on the desk. She sat down again, lifted Max, and rested her cheek against his feathery light brown hair. She said quietly, "I know you hate this, Max, but I have to find out who did that to Daddy. You had a roll to give to the birds in the park, and you dropped it in the car. Irma wasn't with you, there was a different lady."

Was it her conversational tone, the suggestion that she was willing to continue this all day? Max's head jolted against her cheekbone. He said angrily and fearfully, "*Man.*"

Thirteen

On the desk, partly covered by folds of discarded raincoat, the telephone rang like an enemy arriving a little late but still triumphant. Laura couldn't reach it without putting Max down. He made a speedy escape from her, lurching somewhat in his haste like a diminutive broken-field runner; pulled open the door she hadn't quite closed, headed for the sanctuary of the kitchen.

In a confusion arising from the total overthrow of what had become an iron hypothesis, Laura had her hand within an inch of the receiver before she remembered that the study extension was suspect. She caught the third ring in the living room.

She expected either Naomi or Julian. Instead, Delahanty said urgently in her ear, "Laura. Can you talk?"

Although nothing could be heard from the kitchen, Mrs. Wedge's odd phrasing the evening before kept Laura from saying his name. "Yes. Oh, yes."

"I heard about Homer Poe. I have to see you, with no secretaries or relatives present," said Delahanty. His voice was, even transmitted, little short of conjuring: Laura could see the weave of his light charcoal suit, the narrow blue and white striping of his shirt, the fingers of one long

125

hand as he stood facing her with his arms folded. "Where do you Christmas-shop when you don't come into town?"

A mutinous excitement stirred in Laura. "Miller's Cove, about twenty miles north of here. It sounds like a place to buy clams, but there are branch department stores."

"I've been there. Is there still a tavern called the Settle on a corner opposite one end of the green? Good, could you meet me there at eleven-thirty? I suppose it might be wise if you were to buy something and have it suitably wrapped. I have never," said Delahanty with quiet bitterness, "been so devious in my life."

It was a few minutes after ten. Laura, randomly struck by and marveling at her own stupidity, returned to the study, consulted the directory for the telephone company's internal numbers, dialed, and put the question she ought to have put forty-eight hours ago. Yes, answered the voice after a short delay; a repairman had been dispatched to the Fourte house on the date in question. The complaint was interference on the line.

The study extension innocent all the time, while suspicion bred like something in a laboratory dish because the conditions were so favorable. Laura tried to formulate a silent apology to the Fourtes but, however unfairly, found it impossible. The directory's opening pages contained a formidable paragraph about the penalties, state and federal, for wiretapping unless under court order or with the consent of one of the persons participating in the call.

On to the kitchen, where Mrs. Wedge, having supplied Max with his midmorning cocoa and slender fingers of white bread for dipping, was seated at the table with a pencil and an ominous pad.

"A present I ordered has come in, Mrs. Wedge, and they'd rather not hold it for me. I promise I'll do something about a baby-sitter, but would you mind? . . ."

"Max is no trouble," said Mrs. Wedge, furrowing her brow at what Laura had rightly suspected to be a grocery list, "but we're out of just about everything, Mrs. Fourte."

The wonder was that the well-stocked freezer and refrigerator and pantry shelves had held out this long. Putter around among the vegetables and the dairy case, ponder the meats, search hopelessly for things like pearl barley, which stores always hid, on her way home from meeting Delahanty?

No, thought Laura. She said with complete illogicality, "It's bound to be a very large order, so why don't you phone Schulte's?"

Schulte's Market had the only delivery service in Burnbrook and charged accordingly. Mrs. Wedge pursed her lips as if at a piece of pornography. In the normal pattern of existence she was used to being dropped off in the town once a week by Bernard or Laura to open egg boxes and inspect the contents, examine fruits and vegetables for freshness, demand to see the other side of packaged chops or steaks, and in general stay abreast of the local merchants if not one step ahead of them.

"It's the only way, today," said Laura, settling the matter. "Finish your cocoa, Max, and come and help me get dressed."

She had expected opposition after his flight, but he went with her willingly. Had the probe for that single syllable acted as a release of poison? Could even age two recognize that any frightening thing once told was only half as dark and dangerous?

Laura plopped him onto a slipper chair in her bedroom, took out a suit and tossed it on the bed, did her face speedily in the bathroom. Coming back, she said as a casual stage setting, "What was the man like who took you to meet Daddy?"

She didn't even bother to suggest Julian. History might be full of fratricides, but no blood Fourte would ever kill another for any reason; it simply wasn't within their capabilities. Neither did she waste any time on "young" or "old"; a bearded twenty-five would be old to Max.

Laura was five feet six. When she had stepped into and zipped her skirt she walked to a far corner of the room and rose on her toes, holding up her palms for added height. "Was he this big?"

No, in a mute but firm wag of the head. Next, she curved her forearms out in front of her, fingers linked. "Was he fat?"

Max knew what fat meant, and the answer was another no. Could he be thinking that Laura wanted denials, because the first one had gone down without question?

She buttoned her suit jacket and pursued the matter of hair. Was it like hers, nearly black, or—she searched for and couldn't find another immediate example—like Mr. Poe's? Well, how about Mrs. Wedge's?

This line of inquiry yielded three emphatic negatives in a row, not automatic but as if Max really meant them. Red, perhaps? Not that either.

So far, said Laura bleakly to herself as she put on cologne and then earrings, I have reconstructed a bald man of no particular height or build wearing a raincoat or equivalent. "If he took you with him, Max, you must have seen him before. Was he a friend?"

128

The fear and the shrinking were coming back, along with something new: a kind of desperation. He doesn't know, thought Laura in amazement, or he thinks he does but he isn't sure. And, on the heels of that: What about a woman in a pantsuit? And an elementary disguise?

There were too many things against it. It was true that Laura seldom wore pantsuits and Mrs. Wedge never, but he had seen them frequently on guests at the house. In addition, because he loved cars and was denied Bernard's impeccable ones, Laura had often driven him into Burnbrook's center, safety-buckled into his seat, and on such occasions he was a rapt observer. Very short hair wouldn't deceive him either. Even offhand, Laura could think of three weekend-cocktail acquaintances who had chic, shining near crops.

And if she didn't leave the house right now, something would come up to keep her prisoner. Lieutenant Drexel, or Naomi and Julian with the apparent purpose of talking about Homer Poe's death but, under that, to observe Laura closely. If their suspicions were correct, she would know by now that Delahanty had been brought to the attention of the police.

So, the coat.

Laura could not have worn it on this particular day if it had come from Bernard. The large box had arrived at her apartment shortly before London and just after the Pulitzer announcement, when she was writing copy at a department store. There was a note from Robert Gillespie under the taut ribbon: "For all the patient reading, deciphering, and typing. I defy you to think of this as a telephone booth with hair."

That had been Laura's lifelong opinion of the standard

mink coat. This was mutation mink, coolly silver, Peter Pan-collared and lightly flared from the shoulders, as casual as tweed or poplin except for its extreme beauty.

Cinnamon gloves; switch to cinnamon handbag. Max, released from intolerable pressure, gazed with admiration. He said soberly, borrowing an adjective heard often from Bernard but unable to complete it thoroughly, "Stunnin'."

"Thank you, Max." Laura did not have the heart to enjoin him to think further about the deadly figure with the gun. That knowledge, announcing itself only upon the death of a crow, was embedded in him as firmly as bone and tissue. She plucked him out of the chair, kissed him contritely, and bore him downstairs to Mrs. Wedge. Minutes later she was in the Mustang and on her way to Miller's Cove.

The late morning was full of omens, all of them good: light traffic, the sun coming out to flash and tingle everywhere, a parking space opening up exactly where Laura wanted it. Given these circumstances, was it possible that she might escape seeing anyone who knew her?

As a basic precaution, she kept away from the department store and bookshop which were the most obvious goals for shoppers from Burnbrook. The Bath Place seemed much safer; there was an almost identical twin in their own town. Here, she bought a gay pottery stick-to-any-surface ladybug for Max and a sumptuous iceblue bath sheet for Mrs. Wedge which matched the quilted robe already boxed and ribboned at home.

With time in hand, she had both gift wrapped. Then, equipped with the flowered bag like an identity badge, she walked to the Settle.

Even without any etched glass, it was the closest thing to an English pub Laura had seen outside of London. Its long mahogany bar had a roast of beef at one end and a broached turkey at the other with a wheel of sharp cheese in between. Apart from New England clam chowder with oyster crackers, that was it; lunchers who wanted fruit salad or dishes with hollandaise sauce could go elsewhere. There was even a faint comfortable smell of lager.

With eyes dazzled by sun on melting ice, and although at eleven-thirty only a few people occupied the partitioned banquettes facing the bar, Laura did not see Delahanty until he stood up, tall, behind one of the tables at the back of the restaurant.

But he had been watching her. He said simply as she came up to him, "Any fool would have brought you flowers."

"I never wear flowers." To Laura, heart beating nervously because this was the first time she had been alone with him since that other lunch, it sounded gratuitously self-expository. Or, translated into the third person, like the last line of an obscure short story. She said hastily, "Have you been here long?"

"Just long enough to get myself this." It was an untouched whiskey sour. "What will you have?"

"A bloody mary, please." Would they go on like this?

It was a sensible touch that people who had been to the Settle more than once paid for and carried their drinks to their tables, although there were waitresses—eventually— for newcomers who sat and pretended aloofly not to notice that they were the only people there without a glass of anything.

"I had a visit from a detective sergeant last night," said

Delahanty bluntly when he came back. "He knew about my brush with Bernard and asked me if I had or had access to a .22. As it's very provable, I told him yes, and that it had been stolen from the aunt I bought it for."

"Bernard arranged that," said Laura instantly, and explained the line of erasure under the entry for Delahanty in the address book, the information obliterated when there was no further use for it. It seemed a convoluted form of retaliation until you remembered that the Fourtes were circuitous, moving quietly and as they chose.

No wonder Bernard had looked so unruffled that night in spite of his grazed cheek. He had already decided to present Delahanty as a man who could not be fought with fairly because he had a gun. The weapon itself, if not at the bottom of the East River, had probably changed hands a number of times, beginning with one of the small army of people who prowled through trash cans.

"The address handily in my file," said Delahanty. "There's something a little scary about that."

Laura knew what he meant: the increasing bits and pieces of yourself that you left around perforce like keys to a house which gave a false impression of being secure. She said roast beef on rye to his query as he stood with their empty glasses. When he came back with fresh drinks he had also contrived a small plate of cheese cubes.

He said, "It occurred to me when the gun vanished that I'd better provide myself with a more establishable alibi for Friday than looking at old furniture in barns even though I still have wisps of hay in my car to prove it. You will probably be hearing that I spent from two o'clock until five that day with a girl at her house in Corning-on-Hudson."

For all his warning as they stood beside the tarpaulined rocking horse, Laura was visited by an accurate shaft of pain. She took a cheese cube with great interest in its size and color.

"We were very good friends two years ago, and we still have a drink together when our paths cross." A deliberateness in Delahanty made Laura glance up. "Her name is Rose Stuart. She's a free-lance illustrator."

He was entrusting her with something he valued, not the least of it a loyalty unusual in the situation. Laura used the open moment to bring up the issue which could not be left in silence if she were to have any armament with which to defend it.

Still, for some reason, a swallow first of her clean and biting drink; the bartender here was generous with everything, including cayenne pepper. "Bernard never told me that you had been at the house on Thursday."

Delahanty's eyebrows went up at her mildly, as if to point out that Mrs. Wedge and vanished Irma had also been privy to the visit, but then he said, "I'm not altogether surprised. It was over a business matter I'd been trying to reach him about."

With Bernard instructing his secretary to deflect such calls. "A bed of roses," said Laura, unable to help herself.

Their sandwiches arrived. Delahanty said to the waitress, "Horseradish, when you have a chance," and to Laura—chagrined? amused?—"I'll be right back."

He was gone, and at least two minutes ticked by. Laura glanced thoughtfully at his cigarettes and lighter but didn't avail herself of them. A tweed-coated man by himself at a corner table, bony, stylish face lit by clear green eyes, took the opportunity to come over and inspect the other half drink and the other sandwich. "Are you sure this place is taken?"

A merriness born of warmth and sudden certitude made Laura dally with the prospect of Delahanty coming back to find a stranger making luncheon talk while consuming his sandwich. "Very sure," she said.

Another minute, and then Delahanty, carrying one of the glossier home-furnishings magazines with a finger marked in place. "I had to *buy* this," he said with faint disgust, resuming his chair. "Have you ever wondered how people muster the energy to go to bed when they have to remove forty little pillows first?"

He handed her the magazine. "Here you are."

The full-page Fourte ad captioned "The Bed of Roses" showed only the customary number of pillows, photographed like the sheets in a delicate blur. The camera dwelt on the bud carved in the polished dark footboard, the open blossom at the head, the slender arms, which reverted to posts when not in use, slotted and indented to hold creature comforts like reading matter, tissues, stationery, a glass.

What a difference an article made, reflected Laura in wonderment. Although Bernard had cradled the company very much to himself, she had either seen or heard "The Bed of Roses"—but Mrs. Wedge's "*a* bed of roses" had a sharply different context, of irony or anger.

"It was the first design I did for Fourte," Delahanty was saying, "and it came from the heart, or more properly the lungs. I'd had pneumonia, and every time I got propped up far enough so that I wouldn't cough myself inside out I had to bend around to reach something and the pillows collapsed. The point is that according to my contract the original drawings belonged to me after the stuff had been legally baptized and made a public appearance. They bear very little relation to the finished drawings, and they sell as spots. The upshot was that I got them."

Except for the sketch in the study, the airy capturing of joy in pen and ink. As if reminded, Delahanty said, "How is Max?"

Whom he had last seen screaming in the terror of the gunshot and the realization of what had really happened to his father. Dread seized Laura by the midriff. When Max learned a new word, or contrived one out of syllables which pleased him and could be eerily apt, he tried it first a number of times on his own private air, little more than silky breaths of sound.

And she had prodded his memory and driven twenty miles away from him. At her blind snatching-up of her handbag, Delahanty extended a palmful of change. "Telephone to your left and up two steps."

Laura, who earlier had wondered about being recognized by someone from Burnbrook, walked rapidly and heedlessly in the direction indicated, only registering late that the green-eyed man in the tweed coat had looked up as she passed and said approvingly, "Smart. Now you're using your head."

Here was the pay phone. She managed coins into the slot, heard the metallic deposit, dialed the house.

If Irma hadn't actually handed Max over to someone, she had allowed the circumstances that took him out of the park. Would even stout Mrs. Wedge be just as unwitting?

There were two rings, and then the polite but formidable "Yes?" with which Mrs. Wedge had been answering

Fourte telephones for decades, any mention of residences being a jumped-up horror.

"Oh, Mrs. Wedge." Heart rattle not quieted yet; it had been too violent. "Is Max down for his nap?"

"Almost an hour ago. He went off like a lamb."

That allusion leaped on Laura's nerve ends. "I'm just about to start home, I shouldn't be more than about forty minutes. If he's up before then, don't let him go out with anybody, no matter who."

"I would never do that, Mrs. Fourte," said Mrs. Wedge, stern, and then, "Mr. and Mrs. Julian are coming to pick up Mr. Fourte's car. Shall I tell them you called?"

"Yes." Laura was suddenly looking forward to a small confrontation. "I'll see you shortly."

Delahanty had paid the check in that urgent space of time and she poured his change back to him. "Everything's all right, but I have to go back at once."

To someone tense, the flash and spangle outside was like a planned assault. Laura said compulsively on the way to her car, "Max is going to learn to talk one of these days. He doesn't even have to say very much."

"But with every day that goes by he stands less chance of being believed."

Laura examined that and shook her head. "He's a very intelligent child. Nobody could risk it." Ridiculous statement; someone was risking it, so far, and how could that be? Her pace quickened. Oh, God, what about her cover story, her striped bag from the Bath Place?

Delahanty had it, and transferred it to her as they reached the Mustang and she used her key. He said calmingly, "Your housekeeper strikes me as being an extremely devoted and capable woman, from what I've seen of her."

"She is." But what if cat's-paw Irma reappeared at a time when Laura was out, telling her aunt that she had left some possession at the house and bearing for Max a deadly little Christmas present whose powers she didn't know?

The engine caught. It seemed to Laura a delicate cruelty that she hated to leave and could not wait to be on her way. Delahanty, bending only for a troubled glance in at her because meeting publicly had constituted hazard enough, said, "Let me think, and watch your speedometer, will you?"

Yes. While someone else watched an interior gauge with a needle beginning to flicker toward the very limit of "Safety." It didn't occur to Laura until she was clear of Miller's Cove that neither of them had said a word about murdered Homer Poe.

Fourteen

If it had not been for a small circumstance which very few people knew about, Homer Poe's body might have lain undiscovered far longer than it did; up to a matter of days. There were neither newspaper nor milk deliveries; he was out far more often than he was in; he was not a man to inspire concerned discussion among other people on the street.

But he had suffered from a mild form of claustrophia, a fact occasionally volunteered to identities who didn't matter: Pullman porters, hotel employees, a scolding air-raid warden or two in the forties. He had also told his cleaning woman, Mrs. Malcolm.

"It was that window there," she had said somewhat breathlessly to the police, indicating the far one of a pair in the north wall of the living room. She was still recovering from her slipping, sliding, frightened progress up the ice-glazed road to the Cheadles', where she had caught husband and wife on the point of departure to their jobs, and her equally perilous journey back with an uncrystallized notion of standing guard. "I've been coming here mornings once a week it'll be two years in March, and never yet were those curtains closed. I asked Mr. Poe about it, and he said it was his escape hatch."

The two patrolmen, who had called in and were waiting for reinforcements, regarded her blankly. By mutual consent they had all moved into what had the appearance of an office, with files and telephone and a desk where a dining table might otherwise have stood.

Behind them was the living room with its dead man and its door forced by hefty Officer DiMasi. Mrs. Malcolm had never possessed a key, and from the small section of trousered legs visible through a slit where the curtains didn't quite meet, Poe, described by their informant as a man "up in years," might simply have been in the throes of a heart attack.

"It's a sickness," explained Mrs. Malcolm, important, although at first she had been befuddled too. She was a rake-thin woman in her late thirties, with graying brown hair girlishly arranged and at odds with the pouches like clamshells under her sharp watery eyes. "He couldn't bear to be in a room that was all walls and curtains, he had to have a space that wasn't covered up even when it was dark out."

"Claustrophobia," said Officer Ray to his uniformed companion, but Mrs. Malcolm would not allow the ascendancy to be wrested from her so easily.

"I suppose that's one word for it," she said.

Apart from the mild irony of discovery having been hastened rather than delayed, Drexel was not much interested in the little mistake with the curtains. It could cut either way: someone familiar with Poe's idiosyncracy and pretending otherwise, or someone unaware.

The case was automatically his because of its tie to Bernard Fourte. But why had the killer held his hand for so long, nearly a full week? Mr. and Mrs. Julian Fourte admitted to having had Poe's information about Delahanty's quarrel with his employer for days, but said they could scarcely take it seriously at first. Poe hadn't been a witness, after all; Bernard hadn't mentioned any such incident; neither, after his death, had Laura. Now, however, they felt it their duty . . .

Delahanty, interviewed at his apartment at seven P.M., had declined to go into the reason for his altercation with the dead man—personal and without bearing—but accounted readily for his whereabouts on Friday afternoon and was thoroughly amenable, according to the report, to a search of his premises and his car, parked a few spaces from the entrance to a hotel around the corner under some mysterious arrangement with a black doorman.

Granted access to the gun used on Fourte (stowed with a friend?) Delahanty could have streaked up to Burnbrook to kill Homer Poe, but what would be the point with the cat already out of the bag?

Unless there had been other and more unsavory cats in the bag.

Drexel placed two calls to Corning-on-Hudson. As he had expected, Rose Stuart said that yes, Delahanty had been with her on Friday afternoon until five o'clock. Could anyone else vouch for that? "Hardly, Lieutenant. Tom and I hadn't seen each other in ages, and it was in the nature of a reunion."

Next, the local police. They hadn't so much as a parking violation on Rose Stuart, resident for a year and a half—but hold on, said the speaker excitedly, that name had appeared . . .

It took a full minute for his voice to come back, crest-

140

fallen. Rose Stuart, in company with other artists in the area, was contributing her time to a workshop for talented children.

The information fell sourly on Drexel's ear. The girl had sounded mischievous and mocking with her "nature of a reunion," and was obviously certain that her cover story for Delahanty, if it was that, could not be shaken.

As of ten o'clock this morning, Delahanty could not be found in his apartment, and neither was he there by noon. A call to an office telephone number provided by Julian Fourte also drew a blank, but Drexel did not immediately set machinery in motion.

Poe's house showed no sign of forced entry. Would he, seventy-seven, have opened his door after dark to a man he had all but accused of murder?

"I love that coat, it's marvelous with your coloring," said Naomi. Silvery mink and no engagement ring, commented her tone, with Bernard dead only six days. Let's hear your explanation for that.

"Thank you," said Laura, whisking the flowered bag into the closet along with the coat. Around the Fourtes, *qui s'excuse s'accuse* was a very good motto to keep in mind. She glanced at empty tabletops. "Have you had lunch, or can I get you something?"

They had had lunch. "After this morning's ice melted, it seemed like a good day to pick up the car," said Julian, sitting forward in a preliminary way on the couch. He had recovered from a visible watchfulness, alien to him; a search for betraying signs of anger or hostility. "I'm assuming you want it garaged until it can be sold."

"Yes, if you could arrange that." It was a beautiful piece

141

of machinery, but Laura could never imaginably sit behind the wheel; whatever else she felt, tragedy could not be eradicated from leather or polished off walnut. "You've heard about Homer Poe, of course."

"Awful," said Naomi, and Julian shook his head. "Poor old Homer."

As an epitaph, thought Laura, it was both sparse and guarded. She said, "It was a particular shock because he was here just yesterday afternoon. He brought a Christmas present for Max and stayed for a few minutes. We were talking about a friend of Bernard's who came here the day before yesterday, a Mrs. Arpels." Laura allowed herself a small, judicious tilt of the head. "I can't remember her first name, but it began with *H*."

It was like an unexpected center-court shot in tennis doubles, with each partner so sure that the other would field it that the ball was in danger of falling between them. "Hedy?" inquired Naomi of her husband just in time. "Helga?"

They both knew very well, it was on the air, but Naomi's slight twist on the couch to gaze along its length at Julian afforded them a meeting of eyes. Presumably, after twelve years of marriage, a good deal could be done with that.

"Hedy," said Julian, decisive, and ran a palm across his fair head, sending an open and explanatory glance at Laura. "Bernard met her socially somewhere a couple of years ago—she's an interior decorator—and hired her as a consultant on the strength of whatever house or apartment it was." He shrugged her lightly into nothingness. "She didn't last."

"Oh, I don't know about that," said Laura, pensive. "According to her, she came to see what I was like."

"What atrocious manners." Naomi, gathering her coat, standing up and putting on a glove, might have been categorizing someone who had extinguished a cigarette in a coffee cup, but she could not wipe out the tiny electric shock of silence. It wasn't astonishment at the continuing existence of Hedy Arpels in Bernard's life but at the fact that Laura knew. "Julian, if we're going to do this thing, let's do it. You promised Aunt Catherine some of those white hyacinths you've started, and by the time we get home—"

Aunt Catherine of the councils. Send Homer Poe about his business (and incidentally to his death); we will take care of this ourselves. Delahanty's personal delivery of the rocking horse had broken that resolution. Whatever he had to say about the reason for his attack on Bernard, who would take the word of a man who had had his eye on Bernard's wife?

Laura rose too. She said urbanely to Julian, "How is your Aunt Catherine? I hope she wasn't getting weather predictions last night from her arthritis."

"As a matter of fact, she was," said Julian, just as suave, and took the Mercedes keys she handed him from the mantel.

Naomi was at the door, hand on the knob. "Speaking of that, Laura, do you think your pediatrician should have a look at Max? We only saw him for a few minutes, but he seemed quite cross and heavy eyed, not like himself at all."

"His nap, probably," said Laura, "but I'll keep an eye on him this afternoon."

143

And she would, and if his temperature went up again tonight she would have him checked in the morning, even though the doctor had told her that some small children ran temperatures more readily than others and occasionally without discernible cause. In the meantime, she would compromise by not taking him to the park this afternoon.

But she would go; she had to. The afternoon had turned suitable for her purpose.

A half-familiar car moved slowly past one of the front windows and came to a stop out of sight. "You have visitors," said Naomi rapidly. "Let's go, Julian."

The visitor with whom she came face to face when she opened the door was Lieutenant Drexel, and he had come to see them all.

He made no attempt to hide his official chill and the fact that people who gave information at their leisure would be treated accordingly. As the Fourtes were on the point of departure, he would take them first. Where had they been the evening before between eight o'clock and ten?

At home, Julian told him from the hearth. Like Naomi, perched impatiently on a chair arm, he gave the impression of suffering technicalities.

Alone, the two of them? Yes. They had been expecting friends who couldn't make it after all because of an emergency over a child.

And the friends' names? Julian supplied them. Naomi said with cool fury and snapping eyelashes, "I realize that you have your job to do, Lieutenant, but anyone walking into this scene would think we were the accused rather than the victimized. My husband *has* lost his only brother."

Drexel gave her a brief look. The friends' address?

Julian recited it, his arm extended with perfect ease along the mantel. "May we now," he was ironic, "expect a search of our house for deadly weapons?"

"No, I don't think so, Mr. Fourte." Unspokenly, there had been a minimum of ten hours in which to dispose of a gun. A preponderance of murderers were stupid, leaving a trail blazed from motive to deed with items like large sharp knives bought openly in stores where they had given clerks reason to remember them, but that state of affairs did not exist here. "I needn't keep you any longer."

The door closed behind the Fourtes, and while Drexel was finding another page in his notebook Naomi's foreign sports car burst into irritable life. Laura said, "Homer Poe was here yesterday afternoon at about three-thirty"—and told him about the visit, including Poe's parting statement that he was onto something.

Drexel contemplated her with a certain skepticism. It did indeed, even to Laura, sound so very pat as to be false: victim announcing his intention of following a trail of his own, announcee therefore automatically innocent.

She reached for and lit a cigarette, rebelliously. She was tired of resisting temptation, and the smoke would help create a literal screen for what she was leading up to. "I told you that Mr. Poe was inclined to be obsessive about the Fourte family, and he was convinced from the beginning that my husband's death had been carefully planned."

A faint tightening of the official lips; too bad, thought Laura genuinely; she wanted to enlist this man. "We had been talking about the woman I mentioned to you, a Mrs. Arpels, although that may be neither here nor there."

Drexel made a note of the name and address, neutrally.

"I was in from about five o'clock on, but of course, you'll

talk to my housekeeper, and at a little after nine o'clock I called a roommate of Irma Coppinger's, the girl who used to work here, and she came to see me."

"Irma Coppinger. She was at high school with one of my daughters." A very slight thaw on Drexel's frosty countenance was replaced by an inquiring lift of the eyebrows.

"I didn't have a chance to talk to Irma on the afternoon my husband was killed, and after that she was at home nursing a cold. I know she took my stepson to the park, as she usually did, but I wondered if they had been anywhere else. I imagine you talked to her? I ask because she's moved since."

Drexel was not liking this. He had arrived in a mood of general and justified resentment; there had been the elliptical reference to his hitchhiker theory; now, some kind of wispy doubt was being cast on a girl who had gone to school with his daughter. The fact that the girl had worked as a maid in this house might be a tiny thorn in flesh already sore.

He ruffled back toward the front of the notebook, read in silence, said with formality, "The maid was in the park with your stepson from approximately three-thirty until four-thirty, in the presence of Frank Gilman and a blond woman with twins. She was back here by four-forty. She couldn't have killed your husband, Mrs. Fourte."

"I never thought she had." Even in her disappointment that he was not taking this bait, Laura caught the tinge of scorn. The flicker of uneasiness which had given rise to it passed her by. "But"—in her improvising to protect Max, Laura realized that she was actually dealing with fact—"the park is higher in one corner of the north end, you get quite

146

a long view of road. Irma's a cautious girl, and if she saw something that frightened her . . . She did leave town very suddenly, with no forwarding address."

"She probably didn't have one." Drexel's glance traveled around the room. No sight or sound or fumes of traffic here; only trees and lawns. The bronze-framed windows might have been landscapes with white crosspieces cunningly painted in. "Burnbrook is fine for some people, but there isn't a lot of opportunity. I can't see a girl her age happy forever being a maid, can you, Mrs. Fourte?"

He stood up, the subject of Irma dismissed. "I'll just have a word with your housekeeper, the kitchen would be fine, but is there a telephone I can use first?"

Not under her eye, or ear, he meant. Laura conducted him to the door of the study, its desk still largely occupied by her raincoat and Bernard's astrakhan hat. I should have had the wit to go to school with one of his daughters, she thought bleakly. He was not going to take a single step to try to locate Irma, and, with his barely clamped-down anger, she could not bring herself to say the only thing that would make him.

Did he expect her to speed surreptitiously to the kitchen and coach Mrs. Wedge? The day's mail was there on the deep windowsill, and although Drexel had his back to her as he spoke inaudibly into the telephone, Laura dealt with it audibly, contriving a crackle with envelopes, tearing contest offers in half. Could nobody sell anything without a sweepstakes lure? Gilbert & Sullivan's "List" had expanded.

But here was a cablegram from Paris, caught in the foldover of the *Wall Street Journal* and unspotted by Mrs. Wedge or it would have been importantly on top of the pile. "Arriving solo JFK Dec. 21 pm. Don't advise elsewhere. Can you put me up? Love, Marianne."

Although the single throwaway word in there had become as debased as cheek kisses between near strangers, or for that matter sworn enemies, Laura found it warming. She liked Bernard's sister, who had flown over for the wedding so couturiered in misty blue and green that she had appeared to achieve the impossible and be a little bit pregnant.

The twenty-first . . . In the enormity of yesterday, time had become so tangled that Laura had to plot it from the date on the newspaper: the day after tomorrow. In the meantime, have a look at the larger of the two guest rooms, tell Mrs. Wedge, find out arrival times from Paris, although no airline had been specified and on the previous occasion Marianne had arrived by limousine.

And, explicitly, keep her coming a secret from Julian and Naomi. There was something to be talked about in detail before the visit could be sprung as a descent from the blue, and it was important enough to bring Marianne across the Atlantic from a very recent sickbed. It could only be Max's future.

Laura became aware that for a number of seconds—her father's daughter—she had been staring through Lieutenant Drexel, who had emerged from the study. He was there, all right, a face above a suit, but much clearer were four young cousins for Max, to one of whom he would be an elder. For just a flash it seemed possible that Marianne could whisk him away with her at once, far removed from ultimate danger.

But of course she couldn't, and the face and suit belonged to Drexel, looking askance and more than a trifle impatient.

"I'll just collect Max," said Laura, through a sharp pang not caring to delineate him now as her stepson, and led the way to the kitchen.

Naomi had been only half right. Max's silky long-lashed eyelids were more noticeable than usual, but at the opening of the door he crawled out from under the table, where he had constructed a wobbly block-lined path for one of his toy cars, and pulled himself happily upright. His pause at the sight of Drexel, who was new to him, was brief and unalarmed.

"You remember Lieutenant Drexel, Mrs. Wedge," said Laura, which was an explanation in itself, and picked up Max in the interests of speed and departed. She took with her the realization that the housekeeper was not as nonchalant about her niece as she seemed; somewhere in that startled turn from the sink, vegetable knife in hand, there had been a touch of dread.

Upstairs in her bedroom, feeling as deceitful as the understanding and indulgent half of a two-man interrogation team, Laura did not resume her probing, although Max was clearly braced for it in these surroundings. Instead, while she changed out of her suit and heels, she engaged him in a largely one-way conversation about his lunch and asked him carelessly about his mouse.

He knew exactly where his out-of-favor toy was, she could tell—as far as the house was concerned he had the memory of a computer—but he wasn't interested. As if the slipper chair she had lifted him into contained a signal from a hypnotist, he said clearly, "Hat."

149

Laura's brush stopped in mid-sweep. "The man had a hat?" She went on regarding him in the tall mirror, not daring to confront him and snap off his volunteer mood. "Was it like"—don't confuse him over the astrakhan which he had seen on her without reaction—"the hat Daddy wore to the train?"

Ever since his dawning puzzlement as to why Bernard went out of the front door in the morning but did not come back in again, Max had been familiar with the train as a means of separation, and must retain an image of those exits into biting cold, but his veto was brisk. Shrinking down into the chair, he covered his ears with his hands.

A cap with earflaps? They existed in Burnbrook around the waterfront. Or was he simply telling her that he didn't want to hear any more?

Rapidly, Laura put on the bracelet watch she almost never wore and took Max downstairs to the study, but she was too late; the wastebasket had been emptied of its cargo of catalogues, some of them certainly containing illustrations of men outfitted for fishing or hunting. She drew an elementary profile adorned with peak and U-shaped ear coverings, then shaded them darkly because the very blackness of the astrakhan had produced a momentary recoil.

Max watched closely. Pleased at a new game for them both, he took the pencil, said, "*I* do," and made a lopsided square.

But it was coming back, thought Laura. Little by little, details of a scene which he had not really understood until the death of a crow brought it home to him were poking out of a merciful blank. A line from A. A. Milne jumped into her mind: "Hush, hush, whisper who dares . . ."

In the kitchen, dignity recovered, Mrs. Wedge was seated at the table with her midafternoon cup of tea. "Daughter, indeed. If she's the Drexel girl I remember, she was a wild one. You know what they say, Mrs. Fourte, the shoemaker's children have holes in their soles."

So any question about Irma had been perfunctory. Laura told the housekeeper about Marianne's projected arrival and her request that no one else be told, and then, having made up her mind about this on the way back from Miller's Cove, stepped beckoningly into the dining room although Max was under the table providing humming noises for his car on its winding path.

"I have to go out for a while, Mrs. Wedge, so will you keep a very careful eye on Max if anybody at all comes? I can't explain it now, and he's mixed up about it in some way, but I'm sure he knows who killed his father."

Mrs. Wedge drew in a breath like a gasp, hands flying to her grandmotherly bosom. "Oh, Mrs. Fourte!"

"I shouldn't be long, but call the police if anything makes you nervous. I don't think they'd waste any time getting here."

At the foot of the driveway it was impossible in a car to hear anyone calling from the house. Because it was early, Laura did not turn right for the park but left, for the scene of Bernard's murder.

Fifteen

Strange, driving along the familiar road and inspecting it through a killer's eye.

Had that thick clump of sumac interrupting the verge on Laura's right always been there? Of course; it had smoldered red in October. What looked like a friendly spruce-bordered lane farther along on the left was not, although the McWethys had obligingly left a car's-length space in before erecting their barred gate with its firm sign: Private. No trespassing.

Bernard, approaching from the opposite direction, would not have noticed a car parked behind sweeping branches only a dozen yards from where he had brought his own to a stop. All his attention would have been on his small son, plodding along with someone who was neither Irma nor Laura.

There had to have been a car, for purposes of speed as well as anonymity. A few days of observation would have shown that the old road, its surface crumbling at the edges and its occasional potholes spreading and deepening after every snow, was used chiefly by the people who lived along it, but that was no guarantee against a driver of a delivery van or a stray motorist saying later, "There was a young child right around there and right around that time, and whoever was in charge of him was wearing . . ."

A hat, but not the peaked kind in which Max had shown no interest.

Just here, marked for Laura by a white birch growing at a sharp angle, was where Bernard had died. She made a U-turn, glanced at her watch, and drove to the park. Even allowing a generous sixty seconds for the run to the concealed car, with Max carried, the ambush and murder and return to the starting point would have taken no more than five and a half minutes.

The Frank Gilman produced from Lieutenant Drexel's notes as a witness to Irma's presence in the park that afternoon could only be Irma's boyfriend, the "Frank something" alluded to by Wendy.

Let's play hide-and-go-seek, Max. It would never have occurred to him, tunneling happily behind evergreens and rhododendrons, that he had been sent out of the way, that Irma wasn't doing her part. Laura shivered.

Perhaps because she had always approached it on foot before, perhaps because moisture had painted the day, touching dun with gold and gray with hints of lavender, the park looked subtly different. Laura left the Mustang outside the tilted end, the shortest stretch of what was a rough triangle and surely the lookout place, and walked inside.

The stone benches were empty. Someone had been here earlier, because juncos and sparrows were busy on the frozen pond, making feathery forays at each other. That didn't mean that Mrs. Dalloway had come and gone; Laura could not remember her bringing bread for the birds.

She *must* come, she must not today use her alternate route in the daily exercise demanded by her doctor. It was true that on her rests she devoted herself to her correspondence, but like most letter writers she glanced up from time to time, and her air then was detached and observant.

Laura left the park and began to walk around it. In the cold sunlight and gently nodding tree shadows and bird twitters she was beginning to put together something horrifying, something more at home with the secrecy of dusk or darkness.

The house diagonally across the road, dark green, repressive, faintly Victorian, had an unimpeded view of two sides of the park from its upper windows. Why hadn't she thought of inquiring there? Prompt answer from the subconscious: the shutters were closed, and from a banking of leaves against the front door and a generally neglected air, the owners had been away for some time.

A car parked deep under maples wouldn't excite curiosity. People taking protracted leave of their homes generally asked someone to take a look now and then, simply to provide an apparent supervising.

All right, then; with nothing else to do and a death in the making assuming its shape, circle the park, look at the railings. They were bent in two places, almost invisibly against the dark growth within, to a width that would easily accommodate a very small boy in a snowsuit. On the far side, another such space.

Vandals? Every town had them to some degree, with satisfaction derived from the inflicting of damage. Perversely, it usually seemed to take place in facilities intended for public use instead of the country clubs, which could be penetrated just as easily.

A crowbar didn't require real strength or long effort; it was a matter of leverage properly placed.

Laura reentered the park. Say that Max had been thrust back through the railings when he had served the terrible purpose. How sure could his driver be that the car had not been glimpsed in retreat? So, divert Irma's whole attention, that same night, by an offer to help further an acting career.

Max would have, must have been crying, although he wouldn't have known why because in spite of noise and blood he had no concept of death. Of pets, Bernard had said inflexibly, "When he's old enough to realize that they aren't toys and can help take care of them," so there had never been so much as a succumbing puppy. To Max, his father and stepmother and Mrs. Wedge were in a fixed, safe orbit forever.

Still, he must have intimated something to Irma. *"Daddy."*

Irma was used to that. "Daddy's coming on the train."
"Car."

"I'll help you find it." Irma, resigned, because sometimes Max brought one of his toy cars to the park to zoom along the benches and he had after all been out of sight in the shrubbery.

Normality was everything to a child of two. With Irma her everyday self, a little put out at having to push aside leaves and branches in a busy search, nothing really frightful could have happened. Adults ruled, and it was from adults that any important reaction came.

Laura became aware that her own cheeks were wet. For all her shock at Bernard's death and the manner of it, she had been unable to cry before; an interior voice had inquired pointedly, Why this parade of grief when you were going to leave him?

But no matter what he had done to earn implacable hatred, no man should be coaxed into oblivion by his own child.

155

She brushed at her face with her gloved fingers and sat down on the nearest bench to wait. She knew she was banking far too heavily on a courteous near stranger, but just at the moment she could not bring herself to think past Mrs. Dalloway to Frank Gilman and the blond woman with twins ushered out of Drexel's notebook.

Had Drexel ever talked to either of them? Or, in the light of Irma's impeccable credentials as his daughter's classmate and his conviction that Bernard had been another statistic on the long list of daily violence everywhere, dismissed that as a waste of time?

As if summoned by Laura's concentration, flickers of motion past the park's far end resolved themselves into Mrs. Dalloway, entering with briskness. She saw and recognized Laura, waved, and, after a perceptible check, skirted the pond and approached across the grass. Only good manners could be propelling her, an avoidance of what would appear to be studied coldness as they were both unaccompanied.

"Mrs. Fourte." With polite impermanence, Mrs. Dalloway took an edge of the bench. Although her cream and smoke gray hair was lightly blown, she did not engage in any pattings. "It's cleared up beautifully, hasn't it?"

No embroidery of the condolences on the train, no where-is-the-little-boy-today; intent on the functioning of her mended heart, Mrs. Dalloway did not care to open any Pandora's boxes.

Out of a similar necessity, Laura discarded the weather. "I was hoping you'd come. You'll think it an odd question, but were you here last Friday afternoon? After four-fifteen?"

The clear blue eyes did not have to consider; naturally,

156

Mrs. Dalloway had thought of this by herself. "Yes, but not for long. I was driven off by a pair of appalling children throwing a tennis ball around while their mother begged them not to. They knocked over my handbag and when I got home I was minus a pillbox, not valuable except to me."

No part of a bribe after all, but simple accident. For Laura, Wendy Hilliard and her trophy might have been on another continent. She said, "Our maid was here too with my stepson, Max, and, I think, her boyfriend."

"A young man she obviously knew, yes," said Mrs. Dalloway. From her slight guardedness, she had no intention of being caught up in a domestic dispute.

"I don't care how many swains she had," said Laura, as defensive as if Irma had been a member of a chain gang. "But Max was out of the park for a few minutes that day, and it's absolutely vital to find out who he was with. I know he wasn't by himself."

Mrs. Dalloway did some more scrupulous assessing and came to a decision. "Then it's as good a time as any to tell you that I can't help wondering how she can let such a small boy hide for so long in the bushes before she pretends to find him. Oh, I know, it's childless women like me who see danger lurking everywhere. Still, Halloween has turned into a horror. . . ."

It was chillingly close to Laura's imaginings on the way back from Miller's Cove: Irma in her dream world, capable of bringing destruction to Max without even being aware of it.

"A car *may* have stopped on that side," said Mrs. Dalloway, nodding indicatively, "although it's hard to be sure. All that growth has a muffling effect, and those children were shrieking, and in order to be as far away from them as possible I was sitting over there in the corner by the fountain. And of course I wasn't paying attention until my handbag got knocked over and it seemed a good time to go home. The little boy was certainly here then, because I heard your maid talking to him as I was leaving."

If only the park had been its usual tranquil self, thought Laura, or Mrs. Dalloway had left a few minutes earlier. Even in that low-traffic area, it was instinctive to glance back before crossing a road. "Was he crying?"

"I didn't notice." Mrs. Dalloway glanced curiously at her. "I suspect that I'm being dense about this, but why don't you ask the girl? She was probably afraid to tell you at the time that she'd let him out of her sight, but surely by now, and when she knows it's so important to you? . . ."

"But that's just it, I can't," said Laura distractedly. "She packed up and left for New York yesterday morning."

The opposite gaze steadied into something sharper; in it was a suggestion that because of events Laura had her facts badly garbled. "She didn't stay very long, then," said Mrs. Dalloway, "because I saw her and spoke to her in Old Essex late yesterday afternoon."

After sudden violent death, it was like a relatively fluffy bomb dropped through the paling sunlight and filling the park not with noise and smoke but deceit. Wendy Hilliard and Mildred had been deceived too; Laura was certain of it.

In the eight months of her marriage, and in spite of her pleasure in Max's company, she had been by no means anchored to Burnbrook. New York was readily reachable, and there had been Race Week in Marblehead with Bernard's sailing friends, a wedding in Boston, a housewarming in Sag Harbor, a weekend in San Francisco, containing, by hindsight, the beginnings of revelation.

But Old Essex, inland eleven miles, was uncharted territory to Laura except as it appeared on signposts; there had never been any reason to go there. When it had been explained to her that Irma had not been back to the Fourte house since the afternoon in question and there was a reputed talent scout, Mrs. Dalloway abandoned her critical attitude and began issuing directions.

But they were like directions the world over, based on the assumption of the listener's familiarity with the terrain, in which case no directions would be necessary.

"You know where Devil's Drop is."

"I've heard of it, but I've never been there."

"Well, you know the junction of Route—"

"Could you wait while I run to my car," said Laura, urgent because Irma was the key, "and draw me a map?"

Normally her handbag would have offered a pen and any number of emergency writing surfaces, but this was the one she had taken to Miller's Cove and contained only her wallet with driver's license and car keys and compact. Her glove compartment was a storehouse of sorts, and she did not wait for Mrs. Dalloway to delve into her own bag; the Mustang was parked only a fast minute away.

. . . With a man straightening up from a stoop on the driver's side, where he had just closed the door.

He was in his forties, massive, with a beard of close brown curls. His nose was commanding, his eyes gentle, the well-worn gray tweed sports coat over a navy turtleneck sweater the kind in which men grew stubbornly comfortable over their wives' objections.

"Mrs. Fourte?" he said to Laura, who had stopped

breathlessly in her tracks, ready to turn and run again but so far more indignant than frightened. "Bad idea, leaving your car unlocked like that. I'm Bill Sebastian. Delahanty sent me."

"Let me think," Delahanty had said concentratingly as they parted in Miller's Cove, and this was the upshot. No wonder Laura's intuitive lack of fear, although there were other components in that: daylight, hilly space, the presence of Mrs. Dalloway in the park, even though this man might not be aware of it.

Still, putting out her hand in answer to his, she said, "I'm so glad, but how did you find me?"

"Luck, and a description of your car, while I was driving around killing time. Your housekeeper was very unforthcoming when I called from the center. I gather she's a shrewd old bat," said Sebastian with nonchalance, "so the plan is for you to introduce me into the house. I pose as a would-be biographer of your father, sleep on any spare bed you have, and stick to you and your stepson with my tape recorder. Magazines do it for profiles."

Insensibly, Laura had taken a few steps with him away from her car in the direction of the dark blue Buick which was presumably his. Comforting though it would be to have such a large male presence on hand for the next day or two, it seemed to her that an accelerated danger lay in his possible speedy unmasking; a statement to the world that Max was coming almost hourly closer to identifying his father's killer.

And Laura, who could often interpret things Mrs. Wedge couldn't, would be the first to know. She must somehow see to it that she was.

"*Are* you a writer, Mr. Sebastian?"

"Yes. Nature. My claim as biographer will be that I knew your father in the difficult years when he wasn't producing—I took the trouble to look that up," he said to Laura's glance of surprise, "and I had read *A Time for Owls* and I have a couple of the earlier books with me, but if I'm to sound halfway believable I'd like maybe fifteen minutes of filling in first. I've had a little success with the *National Geographic* and we don't want any dates clashing. Also, I'd better know how old you were when and what school and so on."

Wise, yes; twice within the last two days Laura had returned to the house to find Naomi and Julian there.

A wind came flicking along the road, seeming to blow out the colors of the afternoon although the sun remained well above the horizon. Sebastian moved his shoulders suddenly, the ripple communicated to Laura by the fingers lightly, guidingly touching her elbow. "God, it's cold up here. Could you point us in the direction of something hot?"

"There's a roadhouse where they make wonderful clam chowder. Just let me—"

A warmth blinked out of Laura, too, with the speed of a camera's shutter.

"—get my scarf," she said, and walked quickly back toward the park, as careful not to run as she had been on the night of Bernard's funeral when a warning had visited her in the snowy dark at the mailbox.

Delahanty, the open-sesame name. The unheralded arrival, the plausible tale, the beguiling shabbiness of the tweed coat. The expert almost-manipulation of Laura into the Buick with no real insistence showing at all.

Most of all, the beard. It was a word Max didn't know, but even at two he was aware that women didn't have beards, and he had said, *"Man,"* with angry frustration.

Laura swung into the park. Their carrying voices had announced two children even before she saw them, and a blond woman with a toggle coat over slacks was there too, but Mrs. Dalloway, who knew the way to Irma and the heart of the matter, was gone.

Sixteen

Naturally enough. She had already used up her allotted rest period, peered out of the park with some impatience, and concluded that Laura, strolling away in conversation with a friend, was not nearly as single-minded as she had seemed. The arrival of the children who had knocked over her handbag would have settled the matter.

There wasn't time for circumspection. Laura dodged a tennis ball thrown with a velocity astonishing for age six or seven—"That's not nice, Peter," said his mother with the divorcement of a line official at Forest Hills—and made a swift approach.

"A gray-haired woman just left. Did you happen to see which way she went?"

The blonde might have little control over her offspring, but she recognized an emergency air when she saw it. "Yes, I did. She doesn't like my twins, and if you ask me people like her ought to go to libraries instead of parks. She went out that way"—it was the entrance Laura had just used—"and turned down Harkness Road."

"Oh, good, thank you." The scarf folded into Laura's raincoat pocket for that abortive trip to the doctor was still there, and she whipped it cowlingly over her head. "If a man with a beard comes asking about me, would you please say you haven't seen me?"

"Beard? My ex-husband has a beard," said the woman transfixedly. "My God, let's all get out of here. Peter, Chris, come this instant!"

It was clearly a reserve tone of voice, because the twins obeyed at once. Forty seconds after she had disappeared from Sebastian's view, Laura, part of a group and with the Mustang as shield, was tumbling pell-mell into a white Toyota. Was the Mustang even safe after that invasion?

"Everybody thinks he's so nice," said her impromptu chauffeur broodingly, starting the engine. They rounded the corner of Harkness Road. "The last time he came to town I ended up in the emergency room having six stitches in a split lip, that's how nice he is. Is that her?"

Mrs. Dalloway was indeed marching militantly along. Her back did not look promising. "Yes," said Laura, hand on the door release. "Thanks again, I'll explain some day."

The blond woman flipped a comradely hand and the Toyota shot away. Laura ran to catch up with Mrs. Dalloway, who hadn't turned her head. Walking did little for the circulation if punctuated by pauses for chats about the weather, but over and above that she had allowed herself to be drawn into the urgency of a bare acquaintance who had then proceeded to saunter off.

"I'm sorry, Mrs. Dalloway, I got waylaid by a complete stranger. Could—I don't suppose we're anywhere near your house?"

"No, but my car's just around the next bend. This is one of the days I cheated," said Mrs. Dalloway, tranquil about it.

"Then—it's a very great favor to ask, but could you

drive me into town so that I can get a cab to Old Essex, and tell me on the way exactly where you met Irma? I must talk to her, and I don't dare go back for my car."

Laura said it with deliberate restraint, because this woman would frown on histrionics as she frowned on boisterous children, but her sense of time running out got through. After another of her searching glances, Mrs. Dalloway said abruptly, "I'll take you to New Essex. It isn't twenty minutes, and I feel involved by now."

At this noncommuter hour, the crispening air held only the sound of their own footsteps, automatically faster as they reached the bend. There was no reason to look back.

The car was a green Volkswagen, old but as immaculately polished as if it had been delivered the day before. Mrs. Dalloway said inconsequentially when they were both inside, "I thought your maid's name was Emma."

"No, that's because . . ." Laura scarcely heard herself explaining, with equal inconsequence, what would be of doubtful interest even to the mother of another two-year-old. Max was safe with Mrs. Wedge; her confidence to the housekeeper just before leaving the house had ensured that. Even a trusted voice with coaxing reasons why Laura wanted and needed him somewhere would get no place.

And it was Laura who had been wanted by Sebastian or the person behind him. Why risk the public uproar over the killing of a child when the interpreter could be silenced?

". . .do you suppose?" Mrs. Dalloway was inquiring, of some question which had gone before.

They were entering an area which Laura hadn't known existed in Connecticut, wild and forbidding, with huge,

165

savage rocks visible in the thick woods bordering the road in its rises and dips. Hidden water rushed and gurgled, permeating even a closed car with damp and chill. The grape bloom which precedes twilight had already gathered here.

"I'm sorry, I was thinking of something else," said Laura.

"Of course, and I was stupidly trying to take your mind off it." Mrs. Dalloway couldn't glance away from tricky driving, but her profiled smile was apologetic. "Here we are, Martha and Laura in pursuit of Irma. Do you suppose so many women's names end in *a* because of the Latin feminine gender? It isn't a really gripping train of thought."

At the moment, Laura couldn't bring herself to care about the origin of all those *a*'s in spite of a usually preoccupying interest in words. "Mrs. Dalloway, would you be willing to tell Irma—as a preliminary, I mean, because I can't keep you and I will take a cab home—that you've been a witness to her letting Max rove off by himself? I haven't a leg to stand on without that."

"Certainly," said Mrs. Dalloway, "although I think I will take you up on the cab. I live with my sister, and since the surgery she imagines the worst when I'm more than an hour late. . . . Did the stranger who waylaid you have a car?"

In spite of her calm, and after consultation with the driving mirror, the Volkswagen had taken a surge forward.

"A dark blue Buick." Sebastian, car pointed the other way, vigilance increased when Laura left him so hurriedly. Not deceived by her scarfed, averted head or the apparent companionship of two little boys and a toggle-coated woman. Poising the Buick at the upper mouth of Harkness

Road to watch what happened when the Toyota drew to a halt.

He wouldn't dare make a hostile move with two people in the Volkswagen. On the other hand, how many newspaper accounts of road fatalities ended with "No citation was issued"?

"Well, we'll see who knows this road better," said Mrs. Dalloway, sounding almost gay, and put her right foot down.

Although unequipped with anything resembling a whip, she seemed able to communicate to this particular vehicle like a jockey to a horse. Laura closed her eyes as they rounded a blind curve with only the briefest bleat of warning, and opened them again as fragile-looking guardrails flashed by on the descent to a bridge over fast black water with white-tagged rocks in it.

A sign indicating a fork to come: Laura recorded that Old Essex was four miles to the left. She turned in her seat, lifting herself to glance through the rear window; saw the blue Buick starting down the hill; reached a bracing hand back to the dashboard as the Volkswagen took a sharp swerve.

The glove compartment was the kind which opened to the depressing of a button. When Laura took her hand away the door came flipping down and the contents slid out. She bent to retrieve them as the oncoming, lane-usurping van which had necessitated the car's veer went heedlessly past.

A pair of glasses with heavy masculine rims, discernibly clear as she folded the earpieces. A knitted black woolen cap, black as the astrakhan which had given Max his brief fright; from the thickness of its roll-up it was a balaclava helmet. Clinging to the inside, shining against the lightless wool, a cream-silver hair of some length.

Laura put glasses and cap back, closing the glove compartment as if she were reconfining an adder with a weaving head which she had mistaken for a length of ribbon. What had she answered so mindlessly to that idle comment about "Emma" at the outset of the journey? That Max had trouble articulating certain sounds, and had been pronouncing *Laura* properly for only a day or two.

And what had Mrs. Dalloway responded to that? It was there, buried: "I imagine that at his age talking compounds itself quite quickly," and then there had been the rapid digression into the Latin feminine.

It isn't possible, said Laura to herself, rigid; Mrs. Dalloway has nothing to do with anything—but she did not dare chance a second close look at the feet so dexterous with accelerator and clutch. They were shod for walking in burnished russet calf, low heeled and laced, and to Max in his circumscribed world the laces alone would make them a man's feet showing under slacks and a raincoat. Women's pantsuits had jackets. Take away hair and any makeup, substitute a knitted pulled-down cap and horn-rimmed glasses—

Still, there must have been a clinching something else. An empty pipe, long since disposed of? Max didn't know "pipe" any more than he knew "beard," but he would realize that both were male.

Laura's heart raced heavily inside a constricted chest. Beside her, Mrs. Dalloway, whose only reaction to the glove compartment's clatter had been a slight brief turn of the head, said, "Here, I think," and at the last split second angled the car sharp right into a narrow driveway so overgrown that pine branches swished against the body and windows.

They would have settled into place by the time Delahanty's eleventh-hour emissary shot by in the Buick. Safe Sebastian, with whom Laura could by now have been sitting in her living room.

If she dwelt on that, she would not be able to prevent her throat from issuing a sound beyond containing.

Mrs. Dalloway bumped the car briskly up the drive toward an abandoned, empty-windowed white frame house and circled around to its back, the rutted and weedy approach explained by a nest of rusting auto bodies from which everything usable had been stripped.

"Just until your waylayer gets thoroughly off the scene," she said, switching off the ignition, and glanced obliquely across the dashboard. "My sister—"

An examination of Laura's face decided her against pursuing that. "You should have left it alone, Mrs. Fourte. Very young children's memories fade quickly. At two, they're acquiring new information every day, like sponges, so the brain does some selective squeezing-out to make room. Even adults find blank spots in a traumatic experience."

This from a woman who had described herself as childless. Laura's hand strayed with infinite care toward the low-set door handle. She said nothing.

"But not in my case, I'm afraid. Do you know what I was doing three weeks ago today, Mrs. Fourte?" The repeated address had a wound-scratching quality. "I was burying my other daughter. Her name was Ellen. She was Eunice's twin, and Bernard killed them both as surely as if he had strapped the harness on and administered the over-dose of drugs."

Eunice. Max's mother, the gentle girl who had hang-glided to her death. Half willingly? Laura had once wondered.

"But *Max*," she said. She had made the terrifying discovery that the door handle swung loose, as inoperative as a thermostat glued to a wall. No wonder the door had been unlocked and opened and closed behind her so politely. Small fingers might explore . . . The thought of that careful manipulation with a screwdriver swept Laura with cold. "Your own grandchild."

"With those eyes?" asked Mrs. Dalloway burningly. "Eunice was only a vessel. Max is Bernard's, and he will grow up to be another destroyer."

Did the window lever work? If it did, how fast would Laura be able to wind the glass down, grope for and find the outside handle, get the door open? There was no gun in the glove compartment, but this deserted place had been the goal from the beginning, Irma was not in Old Essex, the source of deceit in the park had been inches away on the stone bench.

Mrs. Dalloway—she had made the name indelibly her own—misread Laura's wild and silent speculation. "You don't believe me, do you? You, of all people. Bernard broke his promise to us when they visited us in the South-west, and because of that Eunice got smashed against the face of a cliff. Can you imagine, Mrs. Fourte, why a girl with a three-month-old baby would do something that absolutely terrified her?"

Yes; given an exactly dovetailing set of circumstances, with agonized impulse entering in, Laura could. If she had been initially bewildered by the uncorrectable flaw in Bernard, what about Eunice, sensing another attraction to another woman while his courtesy remained perfectly intact; realizing that the baby, the wanted son, was not going to make any difference at all?

Bernard must have realized the possibilities inherent in the promise required of him, but hadn't paid any attention to Eunice's vanishing at the hang-gliding sight. The desperate bid for his attention and admiration had gone casually unheard.

For someone without a twin, it was only possible to guess at the impact upon Ellen. In Mrs. Dalloway's sparse, clipped words, she had seemed to take refuge in her studies at law school, seeing her parents seldom and withdrawing from her friends. Consequently, there was no warning of her escape into drugs before the night of the overdose.

She has to tell someone, thought Laura with the clarity that came from her brain's simple refusal to believe that at any moment this sky and these trees would be removed from her forever. There could have been no lingering on the road with Bernard, and Homer Poe's house had been a place to leave in the fewest possible number of seconds.

"I don't want to hear any talk of suicide," said Mrs. Dalloway, quiet and fierce. "Bernard Fourte took their lives from them without even caring."

Did that curious lack of lines on the skin come from its having been frozen in place almost two years ago? "So you took his," said Laura. "And then Homer Poe's."

"I had to." Mrs. Dalloway had drawn the Volkswagen up to within a hair's breadth of a hoodless, wheelless chassis, and now without removing her gaze she wound her

171

window down. For the gun; certainly for the gun. "He saw me in town that day after having seen me on the train and followed me back to the house where I have a room. He asked if I was Mrs. Regis Munro and I told him certainly not and that I was recovering from heart surgery. My hair was quite dark when Eunice was married, and I wore glasses instead of contact lenses."

Poe's considering look when Max had appeared in the living room doorway with Mrs. Wedge: he had spotted an elusive resemblance where Laura, living with Max day by day, had not. Then: "I'm onto something," as he departed with his fatal determination to bear Bernard's killer to the Fourtes as if on a tray.

"Of course I warned Regis from a pay phone," said Mrs. Dalloway, "so that he wouldn't answer the telephone until that evening." Her arm had reached casually outside the window. "I went to Mr. Poe's house and demanded that he call this Mrs. Munro, as I couldn't stand being hounded in my convalescence, and he did, and Regis said I was in the shower but I'd call back if it was important, anything to do with Bernard's murder. Mr. Poe said no, that was all right, but I could tell from his expression that he wasn't convinced."

The outstretched coat sleeve was wrinkling at the elbow; the invisible hand would be coming up. Laura's saving incredulity at her own situation began to wear off like anesthetic, letting terror surface in triumph.

The effect was physically dizzying, so that she imagined from the corner of her eye a round gleam of light moving in the woods behind Mrs. Dalloway's intently turned head. She tried to will it into being actual, the monocular of a

172

roaming birdwatcher who would just this once remove his concentration on neck barrings or breast specklings to the question of what two women were doing in a car in this desolate place. It didn't work; she had concocted that sparkle to fend off the knowledge that there was nothing very unusual about getting killed. It happened to people with great frequency.

Say something, say anything, just to keep her panicked heart beating a little longer. "You had Bernard nervous, those last few days."

"Did I?" The controlled mouth tucked at the corners with pleasure. "I sent him the newspaper clipping about Ellen. I was quite sure he wouldn't show it to you or any-one else, not even meddling Mr. Poe."

She was suddenly under the wheel and out of the car which kept Laura prisoner. At her feet, still stirring lightly, was the plastic which had protected the gun in her gloved hand, the gun plucked from the engine housing in a rusty wreck. "Out, Mrs. Fourte," she said, and lifted her chin in the direction of the peeling back door with a trestled kerosene drum at one side. "Regis and I have a place where no one can find us, but you're going to have to spend some time in the cellar."

Could she really mean that it was to be only a matter of incarceration? Of course not. She wasn't a big or heavily boned woman and she wanted Laura's body inside the abandoned house without effort.

Still, having to relinquish that fleeting notion made the late afternoon swim for Laura. She negotiated past the gearshift, throat sick and drumming, because to be pinned in her seat was unthinkable. How many bullets were left in the gun? Two for Bernard. Even granting two for Homer Poe, that made enough.

Mrs. Dalloway, who had taken a calculated step backward, watched her progress with clear, detached, light blue calm. Two murders had not marked her. Far from assuming a face of savagery, she looked exactly like what she had represented herself to be: a heart patient sensibly following her doctor's orders, a woman with the pleasant and civilized habit of resorting to the pen rather than the eternal telephone.

What had gone down on the writing pad, at the outset? "M. no threat as talker, maid poses constantly and looks approachable"? "Have met the current Mrs. F. B. still takes the early train on Fri. afternoon"?

Knowledge communicated itself to bone and cartilage, and Laura's right knee threatened to buckle under her when she got out of the car. Mrs. Dalloway, misinterpreting the fast motion of recovery, said in her peculiarly decorous fashion, "If you try to run, you'll leave me with no choice but shooting you."

But Laura would have to start to run and then fling herself flat and roll; it was the only alternative to walking dumbly to the vandalized back door. The ground in every direction was bare of everything but weeds, as if the metal jungle concealed a powerful magnet which even drew in stones. The woods fifteen feet to the left were the best and in fact the only hope.

Deep breath, then, because she felt winded in spite of sitting for so long, and a prayer without coherent words, and a first reluctant step forward. "You'll have to leave me water," she said on the chilling, dampening air, to brandish her acceptance of the lie, and Mrs. Dalloway said ambiguously, "Don't worry about that."

In the woods, something gave the kind of brisk snap which could not be accounted for by a bird or a squirrel. The voice which Laura had thought to be luring her expertly into a trap said comfortably, "*There* we go. I've got plenty of profile on film, and that remark about shooting on tape, but the full face puts the lid on. Better drop the gun, hadn't you, with the police on the way?"

Laura had whirled at the first word, and there was Sebastian, emerging from the trees which still held dapples of tea-colored light, slung around with sophisticated equipment including a telescopic camera lens and a tape recorder—equipment, she learned later, which went with him on car trips as automatically as his keys. His size and his beard were formidable.

Mrs. Dalloway's small clear features appeared to fall indefinably apart, with patches of white under the eyes. Her gun hand went up and forward. Then, a trace of wind touching her dark silver bangs, she dipped into her pocket, was into the Volkswagen, whose door Laura had left open, had spun it in a tight arc and was bumping fast down the driveway.

"The police aren't coming," said Sebastian apologetically, walking to where Laura stood and trembled. "There's a tarring crew and a flagman about an eighth of a mile up the road, and when they told me you hadn't passed them I doubled back and went too far. I've been over a couple of stone walls, but these are good field glasses and I was hell-bent on finding you just to see what was going on."

For steadying purposes, Laura put out her hand to his,

which was built to scale and reassuringly warm. "After what I did, you were very forgiving."

Sebastian, Delahanty's good and long-time friend, took a forever-private glance at the sky; any suspicions about surviving wives went with it. "Well . . ." he said, and then, "It'll take some walking to get to my car, but I can sit you on a wall when we get through these woods and—No? Okay, no mile records to be broken, but let's chase down a telephone."

If Laura had not witnessed Max's anguished reaction to the shooting of the crow, there seemed every likelihood that Mrs. Regis Munro would have returned to San Francisco as a passenger instead of cargo on a 727, leaving two unsolved murders behind her.

She was not known in Burnbrook; on her sole visit to the town two weeks before Max's birth she had occupied the Fourtes' guest room. Homer Poe and a few other of Bernard's friends had made the trip to the Southwest for the wedding, but according to photographs turned up her only memorable feature was a pronounced dark widow's peak, and nature and scissors had taken care of that.

A family outcry at the time of Eunice's death would have persuaded the police to take a close look at the Munros, but Eunice's terror of heights was largely a family secret, as she was ashamed of it, and the ranks closed protectively over the marital infidelities hinted at in her letters home.

Or was that silence the first outline of the plan that leaped into being when the twin, Ellen, lapsed into her final sleep by accident or design?

The little park (its visiting twins treated with such coldness) was certainly safe enough, and when she was not there assessing the child who would help her kill Bernard and also taking the measure of the maid, Mrs. Munro had obviously spent her time familiarizing herself with the surrounding area. It would have been simple common sense not to leave Burnbrook the moment her mission was accomplished; her landlady proved to be shrewd, talkative, engrossed in the murder, and highly interested in her boarder's figmentary heart operation.

And, at once visible and invisible, there must have been an irresistible temptation to watch from the sidelines for a few days; to see, for instance, whether as a fillip Laura would reveal her husband as he had actually been. Homer Poe had been pure, unpredictable bad luck, but out of instinct Mrs. Munro had hidden her gun in its preselected place.

Or so it was to be supposed. Mrs. Munro herself was saying nothing, the elderly green Volkswagen for which she had paid cash in a nearby town having crashed through a guardrail in her headlong flight from Sebastian and his recorded evidence.

Regis Munro, in San Francisco, embittered and semireclusive after the attacks on his St. Louis design, professed utter astonishment as well as grief. His wife, he said, had been so devastated by their other daughter's death that she had told him she had to get away from their friends and even from him for a few weeks. He had believed her to be in New Mexico.

Laura heard that from Lieutenant Drexel along with his postscript, unimportant now, about Mrs. Arpels' having

177

admitted with some defiance to the anonymous telephone call to the police. She glanced at Max's pink-cheeked Christmas Eve face, thought about a man now deprived of wife as well as daughters, and knew that she would hold her tongue for all time.

"I used to hope for a white Christmas," said Marianne, standing up at the end of the nine o'clock news with its prediction of snow. "Of course, that was before I had to drive."

She had the gray Fourte eyes in a face more delicate than her brothers', and hair that was more tawnily ripe than fair. With her import-export husband being transferred from Paris to Boston, an agreement had been reached with Naomi and Julian, who would in the future have Max for the summer months, plus the control of his schooling; otherwise, he would be allowed to grow up with his four young female cousins.

But Boston wasn't terribly far.

With Max in bed for hours, the rocking horse had been brought in, polished and lively. The Christmas tree was also in place at the end of the living room, the honor of selecting the heirloom decorations having been left to Mrs. Wedge, with bulbs and silver added after that solemn rite. Marianne had brought a beaded white dove with a spray of jade in its bill for the top, along with perfume for Laura and a silk scarf for Mrs. Wedge and toys and a clown suit for Max.

"I'd really much rather stay here than go to Julian's," she said, putting on a slender black coat collared and cuffed in oyster, "but discretion is the better part et cetera, and I have an idea that I won't be seriously missed."

She had been candid about Bernard in the sitting-up-late hours on the night of her arrival. "I adored him, but with my eyes wide open. He was a marvelous brother, particularly to a little girl growing up, but not husband material except to a wife of the same persuasion, and I could tell you weren't that."

She collected cigarettes and lighter, gloves and handbag. "We'll all be down for a visit tomorrow. Naomi will have some struggling poet or worse on hand tonight. She sets my teeth on edge, always has, so I don't think I'll say a word about that captivating man."

Delahanty. At the house once, because he had to see for himself that Laura was safe, and thereafter on the telephone, that contact having for the moment to stand in place of closer touch. In its way, a sweet postponing.

"You can, I don't mind in the least," said Laura, smiling, and, although not generally disposed toward such gestures, hugged her sister-in-law spontaneously. "Merry Christmas, Marianne."

"And to you, and to all a good-night."

Mrs. Wedge was long in bed. She had finally confided her unfocused fears about Irma, who had sent a postcard from New York. "It's not that she's a bad girl, Mrs. Fourte, but that awful thing happening when she was out with Max, and she with her head *and* neck in the clouds—I just didn't know."

Laura went to the telephone and dialed. Delahanty, lurking by his, said, "Merry Christmas Eve, my very dear. I wish—"

"So do I, but there's tomorrow."

179

"And tomorrow and tomorrow and tomorrow." He might have been standing beside her, engulfing her in his blue attention. "I think I'll write that down. Sleep safe."

"You too," said Laura, and, warm, bemused, turned out the lights on the shining tree and went upstairs to Max.